Blow Away the Black Clouds

FLORENCE LITTAUER

HARVEST HOUSE PUBLISHERS
Eugene, Oregon 97402

The names of certain persons and places mentioned in this book have been changed in order to protect the privacy of the individuals involved.

BLOW AWAY THE BLACK CLOUDS

Copyright © 1979, 1986 by Harvest House Publishers
Eugene, Oregon 97402

Library of Congress Catalog Card Number 79-50380
ISBN 0-89081-285-3

Printed in the United States of America.

Contents

Introduction

Many books I've read on depression have been:

> too dull or too deep
> too serious or too sad
> too heavy or too hopeless.

They have shown:

> gloom with no glamour
> life with no lilt
> sorrow with no solution.

Had I read some of these harbingers of hopelessness during my own depression, I might not be around today.

I never intended to write a book on depression. I don't enjoy gloomy people and deeply regret my own long odyssey of cheerlessness. How then did I become involved with a study of depression? It started several years ago when I began teaching a women's Bible study. One day after a study on joy, I was amazed to find the ladies enthusiastic about the help they had received in how to handle their depression.

"Would you be willing to come to my home and give this talk again?" asked one of the women.

I said yes, and my talk on joy soon became known as my "depression message."

On the appointed day I faced a living room full of women who confessed that their lives had not turned out as they had hoped. In a word, they were discouraged. "If only I could blow away the black cloud," said one young girl wistfully. From this experience I learned that there are many women who need their own black clouds blown away.

As requests came in for my "depression message," I began to read and think about depression. The more I spoke on depression, the more women came to me, and the more I learned from their problems.

A lady from England wrote:

> Today I got out of bed feeling very sorry for myself, and I did what I often do when the going gets rough: I reached for your book *Blow Away the Black Clouds*. It never fails to help me out. It actually gets me *doing* things. This afternoon, for instance, I made some scones. (I've just eaten one, and it tasted *awful*— well, you did say failure doesn't matter!)
>
> I've also started corresponding with blind people by cassette—this is something I'm really excited about.
>
> Thank you for your book. It's helped many times.

This revised edition does not change the basic content of the original writing, but updates the statistics and adds subjects such as teen depression, suicide, and inner healing—topics that were not talked about in 1979.

In this book I have approached a heavy subject with a light touch. It is my desire that through the sharing of my personal tragedies and the steps to recovery, you will discover how God's love to us in Christ can bring hope to the hopeless, victory to the defeated, and triumph out of tragedy.

—Florence Littauer

1

Depression Days

Depression. It's a word we heard frequently as I was growing up. Depression meant lack of money and a bleak future. It meant charity Christmas parties and dresses given out by the Works Progress Administration. It meant food handed to us from government surplus and a month when we dined on canned plums. Depression meant my father working seven long days a week in his little store to keep us alive while mother patiently gave violin lessons in the den. It meant that five of us lived in three tiny rooms behind the store where we slept in layered bunk beds. It meant listening to the one radio in search of excitement and hearing President Roosevelt say that all we had to fear was fear itself.

According to the dictionary, depression is being depressed and dispirited. We were all pressed down, jammed into those three rooms, but we were not dispirited. We set goals. We knew we were at the bottom and had nowhere to go but up. We accepted the facts, faced life, and got on with it.

To earn money for college I worked in a department

store selling chocolates and later in a defense plant gluing labels. I studied hard, won a scholarship to the state university, and when I graduated returned to teach in my hometown. With the little money I earned I put my brother through college, and later he worked his way through graduate school to become a minister. My other brother, Ron, became a radio announcer while still in high school and with his satirical wit rose to be one of the most popular radio personalities in Dallas.

With a background of strong family determination, I never expected I would ever get depressed. Always the optimist, I was able to see a silver lining in any black cloud. I married a handsome New Yorker and our wedding was in *Life* magazine. We went into the food service business and worked hard. As the profits rose we bought bigger cars and moved to the "right" side of town. We built a 12-room house and founded a country club. I became president of various organizations and taught English, speech, and psychology. We had two little girls, and finally I gave birth to my husband's namesake, Frederick Jerome Littauer III. Life was complete. I was happy.

But by the time young Frederick III was eight months old, he began to scream fitfully in the night and no longer sat up. His eyes became glassy and he stopped smiling. When these symptoms increased, I took him to my pediatrician, who examined him and called in a specialist. I shall never forget his words: "This child is hopelessly brain-damaged. You might as well put him away, forget him, and have another one."

Hopeless? I could not—would not—believe anything was hopeless. Had I not made myself into what I wanted to be and achieved everything I wanted in life?

"Fix him up," I pleaded. "Do something. This is my husband's namesake. Do whatever it takes. I'll get the money."

With great compassion the doctor looked at me and said, "Florence, this is one thing your money or your willpower can't do anything about. He's hopeless."

The word "hopeless" had never been in my vocabulary. I refused to accept defeat. And when my husband heard that his Frederick Jerome Littauer III was hopeless, he also wouldn't believe it. But when we took him to the Yale-New Haven Hospital for tests, we received the same verdict: "He's hopeless."

Then I remembered the doctor's words, "You might as well put him away, forget him, and have another one." I couldn't put him away or forget him, but I could have another one. It seemed my only hope. During the nine-month wait for my fourth child I began to reevaluate my life. I realized I had put my faith in *me*, in my own power to achieve. I had educated myself on a scholarship, learned to dress myself in style, captured a cultured husband, worked to become a gracious lady, and reached a position of status. I designed and built my spacious home and was a speech instructor at the University of Connecticut. My success credentials were strong. Yet when I held my dying child, none of these achievements mattered. As I held Freddie tightly through his ten to twelve convulsions a day, as I cried with his screams of pain in the night, my only hope was that my next child would be normal and I could put this nightmare behind me.

While I was in the hospital giving birth to our second son, Laurence Chapman Littauer, my husband put Freddie in a private children's hospital, where at age two he died of pneumonia.

With the birth of my second son I became a devoted, almost fanatical mother. I allowed no one to touch Larry but me. I watched him all day and jumped when he cried at night. I gave up all my positions and presidencies—my hope was in Larry. However, one week after Freddie died, I went in to get Larry from his nap, but he didn't respond to my greeting. I picked him up quickly and shook him, crying, "Smile, Larry, smile!" But Larry didn't smile. I feared the worst and immediately rushed him to the same doctor that had treated Freddie. He took one look at him and said, "I don't know how to say this, Florence, but I'm afraid he has the same thing."

We put him through the same tests at the Yale-New Haven Hospital and then took him to Johns Hopkins Metabolic Research Unit in Baltimore. Dr. Robert Cook operated on my Larry and found that where there should have been a brain there was only a round ball, an inert mass. When we put Larry into the same hospital where his brother had died a few months before, life stopped for me. I was no longer interested in my status in the community, my 12 rooms of wall-to-wall carpeting no longer impressed me, and money had no value—it couldn't restore my sons. I had achieved everything I set out to get, but was left miserable and empty.

The doctors told us Larry wouldn't live long, but they were wrong. He lived to be 19 years old and died the same size he was when he was one year old. He never grew and was blind and deaf—nothing but a living vegetable for all those years.

If you are a person who is at a low point in your life, who sees no way out, who is depressed, you may be playing the "if only" game. "*If only* I had a different husband, I would be happy." "*If only* I had a bigger house and more money, I would be happy." "*If only* my circumstances were perfect, I would be happy."

I understand the "if only" syndrome because I spent

my early life searching for happiness. It's true that I achieved a certain peak of worldly gain, but I was never truly satisfied. I was always ready for a new climb, constantly looking for bigger and better goals. I was programmed for success, but the double defeat of two brain-damaged sons threw me into a deep depression. The upward struggle was difficult, but through God's grace and unchanging strength in my experiences, He has allowed me to help other people in similar circumstances.

2

What Is Depression?

Do you ever wake up in the morning with an uneasy feeling? Do you ever fear you're not going to make it through another day? Do you often wish you could shut your eyes and go back to sleep?

Many women I talk with start each day with a little black cloud hovering over their pillow. Some choose to turn over, pull up the blankets, and escape through sleep. Others get up slowly and plod through a dreary day, believing that the cloud is a normal part of their everyday lives, shadowing their every move. Some jump up quickly and run all day to meetings, appointments, schools, banks, and luncheons, hoping to outrun their little black cloud. But refusing to face the problem or accepting gloom as a way of life or running away from the situation is fruitless: We cannot escape; the little black cloud always returns.

One day after I spoke on depression at a church retreat, a woman named Jane came to me. Jane was overweight, and her stringlike hair hung as stylelessly around her face as her clothes did around her body.

12

"I think I might be depressed," she said. "I can hardly get out of bed each day, I don't care how I look, and I'm always exhausted. If I had my way, I'd just sleep all the time."

Jane was depressed.

Gertrude came to me at a church conference. She was close to tears when she explained, "I think my husband is having an affair. He hardly ever comes home for dinner and seems to avoid looking at me." Gertrude was not much to look at. I saw her in the front row and noticed her faded polyester pantsuit with a missing button at the bosom. Her run-down sandals displayed her dirty feet and jagged toenails dotted with old nail polish. In a group of sharp high-fashioned women, Gertrude was out of place. "I don't know what to do," Gertrude went on. "It seems a little black cloud is hovering over me."

Gertrude was depressed.

Lynn leaped up to me after a luncheon meeting where I had referred to people getting depressed when they had too much to do. "I'm really a happy person," she explained, "but I have a million things to do and I never seem to get anything done right or on time. My husband complains about the house being a mess, but I just can't get to it. He'd like me to stay home more, but I would be bored. I'm fine as long as I keep moving and talking to people but when I stop, this wave comes over me. It's like I'm gasping for air. Could I possibly be depressed?"

Lynn was depressed.

Wherever I go I meet a Jane, a Gertrude, a Lynn— different types of women all trying to get out from under the little black cloud that seems to dog their steps.

What is depression, anyway? Can we come up with

a definition? Many have tried, but defining depression is like trying to define love. We all know what it is, but we can't quite put it into words.

David Brand, in the April 1972 *Wall Street Journal*, described depression as the worst affliction of the 1970's. "Depression is the least understood yet most serious emotional illness of the times . . . . All indications are that in the U.S. depression is on the increase."[1]

Dr. Aaron Beck, at the University of Pennsylvania's "depression clinic," says that some of his patients describe their depression as a "wall between them and others. They have lost their confidence in their ability to carry out even the simplest tasks, and so withdraw from the world, and many simply take to their beds."[2]

Dr. Quentin Hyder in his book *The Christian's Handbook of Psychiatry* says, "Depression is by far the commonest psychiatric symptom and it is found in every stage of mental illness, from a temporary depression in a normal person who has suffered a great personal disappointment to the deep suicidal depression of a psychotic."[3]

Dr. Joseph Schildkraut, in a *Wall Street Journal* editorial, states, "Depression is many different diseases all thrown together into one wastebasket."[4]

In *Psychology Today* Martin Seligman says, "Depression is a belief in one's own helplessness."[5]

It is amazing how many people still search for happiness in material and sensual gratifications. The 1960's spawned the *me* generation, the '70's became the decade of depression, and the '80's are called the age of anxiety.[6] Not only are we introspective, depressed, and anxious as individuals, but today we are depressed as a country. We are not depressed because we lack money, as in the '30's, but rather because we have fallen into what the definition says is a belief in our own helplessness and a fear of what's going to happen to us.

As I was growing up, I sincerely believed I could achieve happiness and make myself into whatever I wanted to be if I worked hard enough. The dream of our age was that we could do all things "within ourselves." Many of us still cling to this hope, and yet in this past decade we've learned that materialism does not answer the deep questions and pain of our humanity. We become educated, we earn money, we buy homes and big cars; we get all the things we think are important, and yet we still find ourselves miserable. In a *New York Times* editorial, William Safire said, "If depression is on the rise, where is the sense of urgency to understand its causes and develop preventatives? . . . We can hear the signals and cries for help from the various undergrounds, but we do not listen. . . . But these are good times, this is a happy land. Now we must learn to cope with some of the sadness of success."

Yes, we are sad. We may feel we've "arrived," but we're still not happy. We find ourselves asking, "Where did things go wrong?" "Why do I feel so blue?" "What can I do?" "Where can I go for help?" "Is there any hope?" "Will this black cloud ever go away?"

In an article on "Boredom" in *Psychology Today*, Sam Keen writes, "The pursuit of happiness in a consumer society has left us with an immense fatigue (a national depression) and a confusion of values. We have won our battle against necessity, but we don't know what to do with the victory. At a deep level, we are psychologically unemployed and need new goals and passions to excite our imagination."[7]

We have all tried so hard to find happiness but have somehow missed the mark. While most of us are not hungry for food, many of us are starving for purpose and direction in life. Not only have we failed to find fulfillment as adults, but we have left our children without goals.

An elegantly dressed lady came to me one day in Newport Beach, California, and said sadly, "I think I've raised a bum. I have a 25-year-old son who goes surfing every day, and he seems depressed."

I asked her the obvious questions—where he lived, how he supported himself, how he got to the beach. "He lives with us in a big house up on the hill," she said. "We have plenty of room and I like to keep him around. I give him whatever money he needs, and he drives to the beach in the sports car we gave him for his birthday. He ought to be happy."

Why was her son depressed? He had everything he needed in life, but no goals. Why work when everything was handed to him? He had won the battle, but he wasn't enjoying the victory.

According to an article in *Eternity* magazine, the teens of today find life empty and meaningless in spite of material possessions and opportunities unknown a decade ago.

> The youth of the 1980s—so it was widely thought a generation ago by social engineers like John Dewey—would achieve unparalleled heights. The products of "bigger and better" education, informed of the latest trends, materially and emotionally "fulfilled," and shunning the restrictive beliefs and taboos of the past, they would become the new *ubermenschen*—a model for all time. But, as it sadly stands today, the youth of the 1980s are killing themselves in record numbers.[8]

After I spoke on depression in Phoenix, Arizona, a teacher asked me to speak to his junior high school group.

"Junior high school?" I asked.

"Yes," he sighed. "I've never seen such a depressed group as I have in junior high school today. Most have decided that there's no purpose or hope in life."

A December 1976 article from a Massachusetts newspaper gives details of increasing depression in children. "Suicide among children in their grammar school years, generally thought of as the most carefree and happy times, is increasing at an alarming rate, a Boston-area child psychiatrist says. . . . Dr. Peter Saltzman, director of McClean Hospital Children's Center, indicates that one signal of possible suicide in a young child is depression, an ailment psychiatry did not recognize in children until about ten years ago."[9] Depression, formerly a possession of bored housewives, has spread out first to men and now down to children.

HOW PREVALENT IS DEPRESSION?

Statistics from the National Institute of Mental Health tell us that 15 percent of all adults have symptoms of depression, and this amounts to at least 50 million people. *The Wall Street Journal* says, "Studies show that women are particularly vulnerable to depression, outnumbering men patients two to one." They are not sure how it happens, yet "one out of eight Americans can expect to experience depression during his life."[10] *Psychology Today* reports that eight million people in the United States are suffering from serious depression.[11]

Dr. Gerald L. Klerman, professor of psychiatry at the Harvard Medical Schools, says that as a nation we are suffering "an epidemic of melancholia": At any given time, 4 to 8 percent of the population is experiencing a clinical (medically verifiable) depression. Research at Yale University shows that most Americans could report one or more of the symptoms of depression every day.[12]

WHAT IS THE ULTIMATE RESULT OF DEPRESSION?

Carried to its extreme, the ultimate result of depression is suicide. In *Psychology Today* we are told that approximately one out of 200 depressed persons commits suicide.[13]

In England, after a ten-year study was made to find out what happened to depressed people, the results showed that one out of six had already killed himself. The National Institute of Mental Health, *The Wall Street Journal*, and *Women's Day* have all carried articles that concur with these statistics.

Recently the U.S. Public Health Service made teenage suicide statistics available. They claim that the rate among 15-to-24-year-olds has risen about 300 percent in the last 20 years. The Federal Bureau of Vital Statistics has records of at least 4000 teen suicides a year, but this figure is only a shadow of the truth. Suicide has moved into second place as a killer of young people, following accidents and just before murder.

William Safire writes, "As we uncover our fears, we should take a long look at the perverse popularity of despair. Suicide has now become one of the major causes of death among young Americans. The suicide of a young television star last month cannot be dismissed as the mindless act of an actor who had 'everything to live for,' it was a dramatic and dangerous manifestation of a trend we have been reluctant to put on the public agenda."

The medical profession has taken note of this trend to self-destruction. In the November 1984 edition of *Diagnosis* is an article, "Suicide-Prone Patients: Warning Clues," which states: "When behavioral changes suggest patients are considering self-destruction, don't be afraid of a confrontation. It's best to tell them of your suspicions and encourage them to discuss the issue."[14]

The Mayo Clinic has a traveling medical theater and lecture troupe. They performed *Night Mother*, a play about the suicide of a young girl, at the convention of the American Academy of Family Physicians in Anaheim, California. Following the production, a discussion led by Dr. Richard Finlayson was titled "The Physician and Suicide—Caretaker or Casualty."

We can all be grateful that our doctors are now talking about depression and watching for the symptoms of potential suicide.

3

What Are the Symptoms?

The following depression symptoms are listed in an increasing order of severity, from minor to major. They were compiled from my own experiences with depression and from the case histories of many distressed individuals with whom I have counseled.

One day I received a phone call from a Phoenix psychiatrist. His wife had been at the Glass and Garden Church when I spoke on depression and had bought my tape. The doctor told me he had listened to it, not expecting much, but had been pleasantly surprised. He took time from his busy schedule to call and encourage me to continue speaking on overcoming depression. He concluded by saying, "I just wanted you to know that your list of symptoms in increasing order of severity is right on."

I hope these steps will be "right on" for you too. I also hope they will help you spot the symptoms of depression early, in yourself or in other people. As in any illness, the sooner one finds the problem, the quicker the cure.

1. *Passiveness.* The first symptom is such a mild one that it is seldom recognized. Some men even welcome a new passive spirit in a wife and hope she keeps this agreeable new attitude. But as this passivity develops, the affected person begins to lose energy and doesn't seem to care if anything gets done. Dishes pile up in the sink, beds are left unmade, and dust collects on the furniture.

A depressed man may accept poor performance from his wife or children that he formerly couldn't tolerate. This passive nature may be looked upon as an improvement: "Father hasn't yelled at us all week."

When children become depressed over constant nagging, they may try harder to please and quit rebelling. Parents often see this as a good sign: "Junior has stopped arguing and done his chores. I guess we've finally broken his stubborn will." It's easy to see this first sign of depression as a welcome relief instead of a symptom. When I had to give up two beautiful sons and admit defeat, I stopped talking. I didn't care about anything in life. This silence from a normally chatty mother and wordy wife should have been a red flag to my family.

2. *Loss of interest.* As the afflicted person becomes less active, his interest in life begins to diminish. The *Book of Hope* states, "The move toward depression is a move toward deadness. When feelings that you are despicable, stupid, and unlovable become too painful, you may choose an automatic numbing process—a novocaine reaction—to relieve your pain. However the 'cure' may be as damaging as the cause."

Sometimes in our low moments we want a shot of novocaine. We want to be dead to our problems, yet when we work at blanking out the bad, we lose the ability to see the good. As the depressed person tries to become dead to his pain, he becomes dead to joy.

As I sat holding one dying child after another, I lost interest in everything. I was once a gourmet cook, but now I didn't care if I even ate. I was once a club president, but now I didn't care if the bylaws ever got straightened out. I had once been a social butterfly, but now I lost all interest in afternoon teas. These former activities went from importance to inconsequence. As I tried to suppress my grief, I lost my smile.

3. *Pessimism.* While some people are gloomy by nature, pessimism in a normally positive person is a danger signal. When the winning football coach "knows" he's going to lose every game this season, when your bubbly friend dreads Christmas dinner, when your high school cheerleader won't yell "Rah," depression is close behind.

I grew up an optimist. From three rooms behind a store, I moved steadily up to a 12-room house. I always looked ahead to a more glorious future, until one day I found myself with no future at all. My vision went from bright to cloudy to black. I hoped I would never again wake up, and when I did, I cried in despair. My first thought every morning was, "Is it true?" Then as reality rushed into my sleepy mind, I would be overwhelmed with pessimism.

4. *Hopelessness.* When a passive spirit, a loss of interest, and a creeping pessimism fall into line, they soon lead to a general feeling of hopelessness. An article entitled "When the Blues Won't Go Away" says, "The depressed person feels that nothing will ever go right again." With this period comes a plunging down of self-esteem, a feeling that "there is no way out," and depression is sure to follow. When I learned of my first son's incurable damage, I lost interest and

was pessimistic, but when I found that my second son had the same problem, I plunged into a desperate feeling of hopelessness.

5. *Self-deprecation.* "I am really no good." "I have no talent." "There is nothing right about me." "I know there is no hope." "I can't accomplish anything." "I just don't amount to a thing." When one begins to get this attitude and sees himself as a failure, he becomes depressed. In the *Los Angeles Times* Sandi Cushman said, "Depression, doctors point out, involves feelings of *worthlessness* and *self-criticism*. The depressed person is always *measuring* himself against others and finding himself *inadequate*. He is *low on self-esteem* and suffers from *guilt feelings* because he's not living up to the expectations which others have for him. He's afraid to get angry at others so he turns his anger against himself. *Suicide is the ultimate act of self-hatred.*"[1]

As I sat alone, evaluated my life, and focused on my failure, my super ego fell apart. I had produced two defective sons; I had failed as a mother; I was without hope. When I mentioned these negatives to other people, some tried to bolster my spirit and others agreed that in my situation they would feel the same. For the first time in my life I was immersed in problems I couldn't control. I didn't like myself weak. The plug had been pulled from my power.

6. *Withdrawal.* At this point the depressed person emotionally withdraws from communicating with other people, followed later by a physical withdrawal. A depressed man dislikes himself so much that he doesn't want to burden anyone with his company. A gloomy lady pulls down the blinds, locks the door, doesn't answer the phone, and stays away from people-oriented activity. She no longer wants to be a part of society.

After I spoke on this point one day, a lady came up to tell me she wished she had heard me earlier. "All last week I stayed in the house," she said. "I pulled down the blinds and didn't answer the phone or door. I didn't care if I ever saw anyone again. But a dear friend recognized my problem and made me come today. Now that I'm willing to face the fact that I'm depressed, I can get to work and overcome this feeling of withdrawal."

Once I knew I could no longer be the life of the party, that my sad presence in any gathering cast a cloud of gloom over the group, I withdrew. I stayed at home and waited to see if anyone cared enough to come. Few came. I learned later that it wasn't that my friends didn't love me but that they just didn't know what to say. So I, with my outgoing nature and need for people, sat home alone.

7. *Preoccupation with self.* The depressive person begins to get wrapped up in himself, winding protective layers around his soul to keep from getting hurt. Many women say, "What are people thinking about me?" "Why are they looking at me?" "Everybody is talking about me." "People don't really like me." "I don't want to go to the meeting because somebody is going to criticize me, but if I stay home they might talk about me." This unnatural reasoning and concern for self is another sign of depression.

I had never been a reflective person and was unconcerned with what others thought of me. But as I became more depressed, I began to brood. And as I withdrew from people, I became preoccupied with myself and my problems.

8. *Dislike of happy people.* There is nothing worse for the depressed person than some effervescent optimist shouting, "Let's all cheer up!" This gaiety only

sends the distressed person into the pit. To help him, we must get down in the hole with him and say, "All right, I'm down here. I understand, I'm with you, I love you." Only when we are on the same level can the two of us begin to climb. As long as any one of us has a judgmental attitude over the disturbed person that even implies, "You're wrong, you're miserable, you're negative," he become more wrong, more miserable, and more negative.

I got so I would cry if I heard someone laugh. I disliked anyone whose life seemed to be running smoothly. It was not fair that anyone should be happy when I was so sad and hopeless.

9. *Change of personality and habits.* It's a sure sign of depression when someone who was always outgoing and joyful suddenly just does not care. The good student begins to fail, the neat lady doesn't comb her hair, the cooperative husband becomes irritable.

While I tried to maintain my cheerful personality when I was required to be in public, I changed at home. I went from talkative to silent, from warm to cold, from concern to indifference.

Gratefully, I didn't go beyond this point, but the following symptoms are ones that I have observed closely and suffered through with many other people.

10. *Fatigue.* Overwhelming fatigue causes the depressed person to be too tired to do anything—too tired to take out the rollers in her hair, too tired to get dressed up, too tired to take off her bedroom slippers, too tired to get moving. She prefers to sit on the couch, be miserable, watch soap operas, and hope to be healed by General Hospital.

While fatigue is a common symptom of depression, it can manifest itself in two different directions. One girl who is exhausted *sleeps all the time.* When morning comes and she opens her eyes, the thought of another day overwhelms her and she sinks quickly back to sleep. One lady I talked with slept all day five days a week and got up only to get her husband's dinner. On weekends she kept going because he made plans for her, but on Monday she would be so tired from the weekend activities that she would sleep away another week.

Another person with the same symptom *cannot seem to sleep at all*. I had a depressed friend visit me who never slept. She was exhausted and looked as if she would pass out momentarily, but when she lay down, her eyes would open and her mind could not go to sleep.

11. *Overeating or undereating.* These two symptoms seem like contradictions, and although they are opposites, underneath they represent the same problem. Some people who become depressed overeat. The heavier they get, the more depressed they become. The more depressed they get, the more they eat. The more they eat, the heavier they get. One lady told me she was so fat and depressed she undressed in the closet in hopes her husband wouldn't notice her shape.

Some people who become depressed undereat. I had a girl live with us who was a chronic deep depressant and didn't eat at all. When she was really depressed, she ate nothing! I couldn't tell whether she sneaked something in the night, but as far as I could see, she didn't eat a thing for a month. Her doctor told me she was subconsciously trying to kill herself. Whichever the manifestation, the problem connecting eating and depression is one of ultimate self-destruction.

12. *Increase in drinking or drugs.* This increase becomes a symptom when someone begins to drink more than he has in the past or starts taking a large

number of tranquilizers or sleeping pills to calm him down, or pep pills to get himself going. In an article "Insomnia—and What to do About It," Richard Trubo writes, "Americans spend about two billion dollars each year on a variety of sleeping aids, including new beds, air purifiers, sound machines, records, eye blinders, ear plugs, psychiatrists, and courses in self-hypnosis. The largest expenditure of all is for sleeping pills...[and] physicians prescribe tranquilizers more than any other drug."

A *Spirit of Freedom* booklet states:

> There were 160 million prescriptions written last year for tranquilizers, sedatives and stimulants. The largest percentage of these prescriptions was written by general practitioners, internists and obstetricians-gynecologists. Depending on the drug classification, 60 to 80 percent of all drugs prescribed were for female patients. During the past year, 90 percent of the women seen in hospitals for drug-related emergencies used legal, prescribed drugs.
>
> Painkillers can easily become addictive. Once you start to take pills, you tend to take more and more of them simply to maintain the same level of relief. This is how people become dependent on prescription drugs.
>
> By far, the most popular prescription drug is Valium. *Valium is the single most prescribed drug in the United States.* It is also one of the most addictive. Recently, Doctor David Smith, Director of the Haight-Ashbury Clinic in San Francisco, noted that withdrawal symptoms occurred in people who had taken only low therapeutic doses of Valium for more than a

year. *Twenty million Americans* are addicted
to Valium.

The danger of prescription-drug dependence
cannot be exaggerated. *More people die from
taking prescription drugs than from all illegal drugs combined.* Seventy-five percent of
all drug-related cases in hospital emergency
rooms involve drugs that doctors have
prescribed.

Former First Lady Betty Ford said of her
addiction to prescription drugs and alcohol, "*I
call it slow suicide.* You lose control of what
you're able to do and you can't do anything
about it."[2]

I was once in the company of a close friend who took
12 sleeping pills, ten tranquilizers, and two shots of
whiskey before going to bed. I had never seen her drink
before, and I was stunned. At the time I knew little
about the symptoms of depression and didn't recognize this as a danger signal. Later I found that the
equivalent amount would have killed me, but she had
gradually increased her dosage in an effort to overcome
her depression and go to sleep. She ended up spending
a year in a mental hospital, and now I regret that I didn't
know how to take some corrective action.

13. *Poor concentration.* It's obvious that after going
through all of these previous stages, the depressed
person cannot really get it all together. Everything in
life seems blurred. It's extremely difficult for a disturbed person to think clearly, and it is therefore unwise
for him or her to make big decisions. One's lack of clear
vision can lead to mistakes that would never normally
be made.

14. *Hypochondria.* Many extreme depressants

ultimately just take to their beds. If up to this point they have been to all the doctors, and everyone has said it is all in their heads, and no one will agree with them that they are sick, they may just give up and shut themselves in their room. Then somebody has to pay attention.

When the depressed person quits trying and is constantly ill, we must realize that this represents a desperate cry for help. Once a person believes that no one understands him, he begins to seek a way out. Some settle in as invalids and get a perverse pleasure from having other people care for them. Others decide that life in bed is too depressing and look for a way to end it all.

15. *Suicidal tendencies.* "To be or not to be—that is the question." By the time the depressant has come this far, he begins to seriously debate whether there is any use in living at all. One girl told me, "I have decided my husband would be better off if I were dead." A broken man told my husband he prayed that God would make him a corpse. Some people say, "I've been dead for years; now all I have to do is dispose of the body." "I might as well get it over with." "There's nothing left to live for." We need to take positive steps with serious statements like this, and assure the person that he is being heard. Most cities have suicide prevention centers listed under Suicide or Crisis, and there is help available through local mental health centers, emergency rooms, or community family counseling services.

Said one lady, "I have come to this talk too late. My teenage son went through all the steps you listed. He had talked of suicide and I passed it off as a bid for attention. A few weeks ago he shot himself. He was just 16."

Dr. Quentin Hyder says, "Eight out of ten suicides

have talked about it before.''[3] Listen well!

16. *Sudden improvement.* Sometimes the extreme depressant will take what appears to be an encouraging turn for the better. I saw this happen before I understood the symptom. Jane and Jim had been college sweethearts: she, the head cheerleader and he, the captain of the football team. After their wedding they had four children in as many years and she became depressed. No longer did she look like a beauty queen, and she expressed dislike for her children.

I visited her one day and she appeared to be better. The children didn't seem to bother her; she smiled and ignored their crying. Later I told my husband that I thought Jane had finally gotten things under control. The next day she stabbed herself with a butcher knife and was taken to the mental hospital. Later the doctor told me that when she seemed to improve, she had really decided to kill herself and so nothing mattered anymore. A sudden improvement after a long depression may be a sign that the planned end is near.

One young lady came up to me after I cited this case in a talk on depression and told me about her mother. After months of withdrawal from everyone, initially caused by the death of her husband, this lady called her three daughters and invited them and their husbands to dinner. She had candles and crystal on the table, served a gourmet meal, and was elegantly dressed.

They all enjoyed the dinner, and as they left for their homes, each commented how pleased they were that their mother had finally snapped out of her depression and seemed herself again. But it was only a ruse. The dinner was her own farewell party. That night she ended her loneliness by taking an overdose of sleeping tablets.

A teenage girl in Arizona, depressed from her

mother's remarriage because she felt left out and lonely, quickly went down the steps to despair. She became preoccupied with death and wrote an essay for her English class entitled "The Welcome at the Top of the Stairs." She developed the theory that in heaven she would get the recognition and love she felt she missed on earth. The teacher gave her an A, but did not recognize her plea for help. Later the girl's mother told how her daughter had smiled for the first time in months as she showed everyone her A. The family congratulated her, although no one took the time to read the essay. Two days later her mother went in to wake her and found her dead. Beside her was an empty bottle of sleeping pills and in her hand the essay with the A. It is important to realize that *a sudden improvement after a long period of depression may mean the end is near.* Dr. Victor M. Victoroff writes to the medical profession, "Beware of a sudden lifting of the patient's depression; it may signal relief over finally having decided to commit suicide, providing the energy to carry out the act."[4]

17. *The call to death.* The last step before suicide is when the depressant wills himself out of reality. He has programmed himself to be in a position where he is beyond it all—in another world, and where he is ready to go to a further world.

A girl named Sandra told me about her husband. "I don't know what's the matter with him. He doesn't seem to know I exist." As I questioned her, she unconsciously laid out a perfect pattern of depression. Alan had been married before. He had been through a "nasty divorce" and had lost his house, car, and boat. His payments to his first wife were so high that he had little left to live on. When he married Sandra, he appeared happy and well-adjusted, but his financial problems soon surfaced and he needed her income to pay the rent.

Sandra had her own business, and she soon found herself supporting the two of them while he supported his first family. When she mentioned this problem to him, he became negative and stopped talking to her. Next he lost interest in his job and said, "Why bother working? I don't get to keep any of it anyway." His comments became increasingly pessimistic, and he kept mumbling about the hopeless mess he was in.

When Sandra tried to communicate with him, he would reply, "Why do you want to talk with me? I'm a failure, you're a success. You'd be better off without me."

The more Sandra tried to cheer him up, the more he withdrew from her. One day when she was telling him a funny incident from her work, he hit her and yelled, "Take that smile off your face!"

He was always exhausted and stopped working around the house. When he came home at night he went straight to bed without dinner. Sandra tried to bring him food, and one night he kicked the tray off the bed and sobbed, "I don't ever want to eat again."

"To make matters worse," said Sandra, "this week he was demoted at work and now he walks around like a zombie. A concerned friend arranged to meet him for lunch today, but he didn't show up. In fact, he didn't even go to work today. He went out and left me a note saying, 'Dear Sandra, It's not your fault. I should never have married you. My life is hopeless and you'll do better without me.' "

A few years ago a deeply depressed friend came to visit me. She had reached the point of detachment; she would sit by the hour holding a magazine upside down before her. I could speak to her, wave at her, or take the magazine away, and she wouldn't change her expression. Later she told me, when her suicide was averted, that she was already in another world and was dreaming of what heaven would be like. A girl I dealt with in San Francisco heard voices at this step encouraging her to come to a place of eternal rest. Another saw angels when she closed her eyes.

A Filipino poet employed as a taxi driver jumped off the Golden Gate Bridge with his niece. His suicide note, as reported in several newspapers, said, "Perhaps this life has been too vivid for my spirit. I know there are distinctions within and without. Something has called my being and I can just not refuse the offer." He had felt the call of death and had jumped off the bridge backward, holding hands with his niece. In a poem called "What We Know" Bayani Mariano wrote:

> When I have seen this circumstance
> and that failing
> And all the past colors turn and twist—
> all that have been;
> I am all at once like a spectator,
> waiting for something.

The ultimate symptom of depression is the call to end it all.

If you are fortunate enough to be free of depression yourself, it is still important for you to understand the symptoms so that you can be compassionate with other people.

4

Who Gets Depressed?

Now that we have seen the symptoms, let's ask, "*Who gets depressed?*" Does everyone get depressed? From the following list, we can see that anybody *could* get depressed. Let's first look at the person who begins his life with a big black cloud over his head—the proverbial born loser.

1. *The born loser* starts life knowing he is hopeless. He throws his bottle out of the crib and his mother yells, "You dummy, don't you know this is new carpeting?"

The chubby toddler trips, and the visiting aunt says, "I hope she won't be fat and clumsy *all* her life."

The first-grade teacher states, "You're the *only* one in class who can't tell red from green."

The second-grade teacher asks, "Why aren't you *smart* like your brother?"

The third-grade teacher sighs, "Can't you ever keep your mouth *shut*?"

The mother looks at the report card and screams, "A 'D' in reading? *My* child?"

The father tells his uncoordinated son, "When I was your age, I was captain of the baseball team."

Did anyone ever say things like this to you? Have you ever made similar statements to other people?

I once talked with a young man who told me his mother nicknamed him the Blob when he was a baby. She told everyone how quiet he was and how he did nothing. When he started Sunday school, she became his teacher. "He wouldn't know how to respond to anyone else," said the mother. "He needs me." Each year they moved up together. She walked him to school through eighth grade and cut up his food until he was in high school. Without her he could do nothing. Today at 30 he is ill at ease with her constant instructions, yet helpless without her. In her mind she was a devoted mother, but she has produced a loser.

A lovely bride came to me in tears, exclaiming that she would never be able to cook. This seemed to me a simple problem to solve until the bride told me her mother never let her in the kitchen. She had told her she was too young, too dumb, too slow, too messy, and too clumsy—and always ended by saying, "I can do it faster myself if you'll just stay out of the way."

One depressed young man told me his mother always said to him, "I hope you have a son just like you when you grow up so you'll know what I went through."

Comments like these insure that our children will grow up depressed. The responsibility in this area lies with us. If we bring up our children to believe that they're no good, insignificant, and inferior, and that they don't measure up to others, we'll program our children to be losers. Once a child gets the idea that he can't make it or can't do it, he won't bother trying. He'll fall into a pattern of hopelessness. One of the first signs of depression in a child is when he or she begins

to give up and no longer cares to enter into normal social activity or feels he can't do anything.

Be careful not to heap negatives on your children, and whenever you see a child being programmed toward depression, step in and do something for him. If you can't share with the mother, then try to work with the child, building him up in a positive way. Help him to set goals in his life; encourage the child to verbalize his problem and get his frustrations out in the open. *A born loser is programmed for depression.*

2. *Successful people* can have a tendency toward depression, especially the person who has reached the top and has no more exciting plans ahead. Dr. Beck in *The Wall Street Journal* says, "They reach the pinnacle of achievement, their goal in life, and suddenly they realize there is nothing left to achieve. The result is depression."[1]

A brilliant New York banker jumped out of a 30-story window. He left a note saying he had achieved success and there was nowhere left to go. When we have no daily purpose in life, we become depressed. It was Robert Browning who said, "A man's reach should exceed his grasp, or what's a heaven for?"[2] So many of us spend our lives waiting to be happy, waiting until we receive everything we have aimed for so we can finally relax and enjoy ourselves. *If only* I had this or that, I could be happy. Such a preoccupation is to waste one's life. We need goals; we need a reason to get up each day; we need a cheerful attitude toward our work. "Where there is no vision, the people perish."[3] Don't wait to be happy until you reach the mountaintop. Enjoy the climb.

One lady came to me after listening to my "depression message" and said in shock, "I'm afraid my husband is depressed!" He had been a business executive

in a national company and had recently retired. He had always been aggressive and demanding and she had feared having him at home. Contrary to her expectations, he was quiet and uncritical. She felt this change of personality a blessing until we went over the symptoms and she saw he was already in the withdrawal step. She had been so glad he wasn't picking on her that she hadn't noticed his loss of interest in life around him. Later, when she discussed his silence with him, he wept and said, "I didn't think you even cared." Together they established goals to replace the constant aims he had enjoyed at work, and his depression disappeared. An article for doctors points out that a high-risk group for suicide would be "physicians and other professionals at the peak of their careers who are substance-abusers, overly self-critical, or have suffered recent humiliation or tragic loss."[4]

A nurse who was about to retire knew she would become depressed. "It's straight downhill from here, and I don't know what to do about it." As we reviewed her need for new purpose in life, she brightened up and promised she would look for new horizons. Within a week she met the director of a convalescent hospital who desperately needed part-time help. She went from one job to the next and soon organized a volunteer program which grew rapidly under her direction. No matter what our age we need challenges to make each day worthwhile. *No purpose = no accomplishment = depression.*

3. *Those who cannot communicate.* Why do some of us grow up unable to communicate? As I talk to teenagers today, I find several clues. Some tell me their mothers seldom let them finish a sentence, so they quit talking. Many complain that whatever they say, their parents tell them it's stupid. My daughter had a

boyfriend who told her he got nervous when eating dinner at our house. When she asked him why, he said it was because we all talked so much and he didn't know what to say. When she ate at his home, she found the reason for his inability to communicate: They all ate in front of the TV and no one said a word.

There was no TV when I grew up, and we had to talk to each other. My father led our mealtime discussions on current events. Words were important to us, and a witty retort brought appreciative laughter. In contrast today, our thinking and speaking is done for us by actors who are paid by a soap company to baby-sit. Many of our children have become passive observers of lust and life, and the less we hear about it, the better. A 1985 survey by *U.S. News and World Report* says, "During grades 7-12 kids listen to an average of 10,500 hours of rock music. During grades 9-12 they see 18,000 murders in 22,000 hours of TV, twice the time they spend in twelve years of school."[5]

Are you allowing your children to be amused by the media because it's easier than spending time with them in meaningful conversation? If we don't guide our children into a positive pattern of conversation, they will grow up unable to communicate, unable to share their feelings, and carrying deep bottled-up resentments.

My husband and I once had a couple come to us who were full-time Christian workers but confessed they had no meaningful relationship with their two teenagers. We gave them a set of questionnaires we had devised to help parents and teenagers open up problem areas and suggested that after the test they sit down and lovingly share their answers with each other. "Some of the responses may hurt," we said, "but listen attentively and don't interrupt." We never heard from this couple again, but one day six months later I met the wife in the supermarket. "I'm so embarrassed to see you," she said. "We've just never had the time to sit down with our children and do that nice little test you gave us."

They *never* had time for their children, who felt isolated from their parents. In desperate bids for attention, their son got a girl pregnant and abandoned her on his mother's doorstep while he escaped into the army. The daughter, after attempting suicide, stole a car and disappeared—all because the parents couldn't find time to communicate with their children.

Do you have time for your children? Do you have meals together as a family where you encourage your children to talk, uninterrupted and uncriticized? Do you share with them your burdens and ask their help and suggestions? Do you keep your family up-to-date on the news of the day?

As I was raising my children, each morning after breakfast I would skim quickly through the newspaper while the children were getting ready to leave for the day. I would then present brief reviews which would give them current conversational topics appropriate to their activities. They loved mother's "little gems" and had fun working today's facts into their daily dialogue. Every minute we spend in meaningful conversation with our children will add to their adult ability to communicate. *Those who cannot communicate become depressed.*

4. *Those who can't compete.* Many parents overprotect their children to the point where the child doesn't understand that life is real. Such a child believes that his mother will run interference for him forever. He has never learned to get in there and "fight it out."

When my daughter Marita was in nursery school, she

refused to go to her graduation. It was a prestigious school where the final ceremony was a noted event in the community, and I was eager to be present. But the more I pleaded, the more adamant she became. At this point in my life I was very concerned over the eyes of the world, so I *had* to show up at the graduation. Besides, I had bought her an expensive ruffled dress and was not about to waste it. As I begged her to go, she finally gave me her reason for refusal. All the little children were going to be in a potato race, and every time she practiced, she dropped her potato. Since she couldn't win, she was *not* going to enter.

I called the teacher, had Marita removed from the potato race, and went out proudly to the graduation. Later, with the wisdom of the Lord, I began to notice that Marita was making anything unpleasant in life into a potato race, and I was constantly protecting her from facing reality. It was difficult for me to let my little doll stand up for herself, fight her own battles, and learn to compete alone, but I had to force her to grow up.

When we make things too easy for our children, either on purpose ("so he won't have to go through what I went through") or by benign neglect ("It was easier to just do it for her than teach her."), we do them a great disservice in the guise of charity, and we unknowingly encourage a dependency personality which may turn them to drugs or alcohol.

In my book *Lives on the Mend* I tell the story of Paulette, whose mother did everything for her, firmly believing that this was a positive program for Paulette's life. The mother desperately needed to be needed, and by her slavish devotion to her child she bound the girl to her in a dependency situation. While this sacrificial behavior may appear laudatory, it produces young adults who don't know how to compete when they enter the real world. They either return to mother, find some other person who will care for them in what may become a sick relationship, or (as Paulette did) start to drink and become dependent on alcohol or pills.

What is now called the "dependency personality" starts in childhood when a child is not taught responsibility, does not learn how to compete, and thinks that Mother will always sweep ahead, parting the Red Seas of life.

We parents have to realize that our goal is not to have our children cling to us forever, professing their need for protection, but to bring them up in such a way that they will be able to face life without us. Are you overprotecting your child? Is the teacher always wrong, the employer always a villain, the policeman always vindictive? *Those who cannot compete give up and become depressed.*

5. *Those with too much to do.* I have always had too much to do. This area of constant activity gets me discouraged. Gratefully, my husband has learned to protect me in this way. When he sees that I am overwhelmed, he will sit down with me and say, "Let's make a list of what you have to do." Then he shows me that I don't need to go to the Literary Club and sit through a book review when I have no time to read a book, that I don't need to attend a fashion show when my closet is bulging, that I don't need to present my bylaw amendment in person when I can mail it to the parliamentarian.

Thankfully, my husband has taught me that I'm not indispensable: The community will continue without my eager eye and active tongue. As I talk with depressed women, I find many who are so involved in civic and social activities that they have no time for their families. Some women know their priorities are out of order but seem trapped by peer pressure.

Many women I meet are so busy with church activities and doing good works that they have little time for their homes. These same women have the prayer chains pleading with God that the husbands will become wonderful Christians like they are!

Do the demands of your outside activities keep you from making beds? Are you an expert at emergency suppers? Are your children becoming TV dinner addicts? Do you take it out on your husband when you are snubbed at the women's club?

We must analyze our lives to make sure our priorities are in correct order. *Exhaustion leads to depression.*

6. *Those with nothing to do.* Having seen that those with too much to do get discouraged, you might think it a contradiction that those with nothing to do are also depressed and easily bored. I've talked with many disturbed women who see no reason to get up in the morning. One day a young woman who lived in a big house with a Mercedes in her garage phoned me and told me she was lonely and bored. I later phoned a friend who taught a Bible study and asked her to see if she could get the girl involved.

"We all know she's lonely," said my friend, "and we've invited her to many group activities. She says she'll come, but when we go to pick her up, she refuses to budge." Here is a depressed girl with nothing to do who nevertheless refuses help from other people. One of the fastest ways to head downhill into deeper depression is to sit and do nothing.

In contrast, I know many elderly people, some who live alone, who find life active and purposeful. When my mother was in her eighties she lived in a senior citizens' village in Massachusetts, arose each morning at 7:00, made herself a good breakfast, and then kept herself busy with Red Cross work and a craft program at her church. She often had friends in for supper and was a cheerful member of her activity groups. She took good care of her physical and mental health, looked far younger than her years, and died peacefully in her sleep at 85.

There are so many groups who need volunteers, so many phone calls to be made, so many lonely people to visit, so many Bible studies to attend that no one needs to feel lonely or purposeless.

A widow in Columbus, Ohio, came to our Christian Leaders And Speakers Seminar there and expressed to me that there was no reason for her being there except to please her daughter. Her husband had been a pastor and the district superintendent of their denomination. With his death her entire world had collapsed, and without him she felt totally useless. I told her about the tremendous need for a woman to minister to widows and suggested that she think of ways to help these other women out of their depressions.

Her response to my challenge was different from what I had expected. She started calling women and inviting them to attend whatever I was doing in the state of Ohio. More than inviting, she insisted that they come. Now everywhere I appear in the state, there is Mrs. Tucker with a group of ladies! As she introduces me to each one, I learn that some have flown in from New York or Florida and that she is the catalyst for these gatherings. I've told her I wish I could afford to send her ahead of me all over the country as a public relations person!

Instead of feeling that life is over, Mrs. Tucker is now lifting up the spirits of her friends. Her daughter Monda told me, "I can't believe the difference in mother since she organized the Florence Littauer Fan Club!''

Do you find it easier to stay home and feel lonely than to get up and participate in life's adventures? Do you wait for people to come to you and then get upset when no one shows up? Do you skip meals because it's not worth the effort to cook for just one person? Any of these attitudes can breed pessimism. The next time you begin feeling sorry for yourself, find someone worse off than you are and try to cheer him up. You'll come away renewed in your spirit!

I heard of an elderly Christian lady who was confined to her home with an incurable disease. Instead of becoming depressed, she began to pray for a few speakers she knew. She asked them to keep her posted on their schedules and promised to uphold them in prayer during the times they ministered. The speakers began to call her and send cards from their travels. As they shared with friends how this lady prayed for them, others began to phone in requests. Soon she had a network of Christian speakers keeping in touch with her and sharing their answers to her prayers. What could have been a life of despair became one of daily excitement. *Boredom is the baby of depression.*

7. *Those in drastic circumstances.* Many people suffer such tragedies in their lives that there is an obvious reason for deep depression. Mary discovers her husband is having an affair. Hazel's mother just died. Sally's child was hit by a motorcycle. Barbara's car was totaled by a drunken teenager. Jerry's 14-year-old daughter is pregnant. I had two sons with hopeless brain damage. These types of problems produce understandable depression and are difficult to overcome in our own strength.

In 1967 Drs. T. H. Holmes and R. H. Rahe rated the varying amount of stress caused by certain specific changes in the lives of 5000 of their patients. They gave each stress a specific point value. The death of a spouse is 100 points, divorce is 73 points, separation is 65 points, jail is 63 points, etc. This stress analysis shows the kinds of circumstances we meet in life and the drastic effects they have on us.

In dealing with people in critical circumstances, I have learned that *the first step must be an acceptance of the fact.* Only when we realistically face the truth can we begin to overcome the hurt and despair. The worst approach is to pretend it never happened.

Recently at a women's retreat one of the leaders painfully told me her husband had left her. She was miserable, heartbroken, and humiliated. As we talked, I found that she was unwilling to face the truth and honestly deal with her future. She called him frequently at work, wrote him, and begged him to take her out. But all that these pleadings brought forth was a further revulsion for the woman he had cast aside.

I've found that when a woman in this position is willing to face her situation squarely, pull herself together, and get on with a positive plan for life, her husband often sees a new and attractive side of her and returns. In contrast, I have yet to see a man return because of a wife's wailing.

The death of a loved one is devastating, but in due time life must go on. We must face it, sorrow for a season, and then get on with life. One family I know continues to sorrow over the death of a 70-year-old father and husband. For three years Nancy has called her mother each day to see "how she's taking it." When the mother cries, Nancy hastens over and they drive to the cemetery, where they both weep. As each holiday approaches they make life miserable for the whole family by mourning that this is the third Easter without

Father. By perpetuating an eternal funeral, they keep themselves and everyone else depressed.

In my daughter Lauren's book *What You Can Say. . . When You Don't Know What to Say* she gives practical advice on how to minister to those who are hurting. The first step is to acknowledge the loss, the second to allow the person to grieve in whatever way they find appropriate, and third to ultimately help them to a healthy resolution of the situation and emotions. Lauren includes a helpful chart showing you what to say and not to say in different types of difficult and traumatic events. *Drastic circumstances can put us into constant depression.*

8. *People with serious illness.* In the year 1985 much attention was given to "mercy killing" or helping the elderly with fatal diseases to commit suicide. Betty Rollins has a new book on the bestseller list, *The Last Wish*, giving the steps she went through in helping her mother to commit suicide. The HEMLOCK Society is promoting the legalized use of lethal injections by doctors for the terminally ill who desire to die.

A doctor I know found out he had cancer. He had observed the languishing deaths of many of his own patients, and he couldn't face the thought of going through this anguish himself. He finished his rounds for the day, then went home and shot himself.

While pregnancy is not a terminal illness, and illegitimate children are not the disgrace they used to be, some teenagers look at the nine months as a slow death and commit suicide rather than humiliate their families. *When life as it is seems hopeless, suicide seems to be a positive alternative.*

9. *Those with a low self-image.* While a correct self-image is desirable, many people grow up with a low self-image. They feel they can't do anything right, they

don't look good, or they never know what to say. This poor view of themselves is often instilled by parents who repeatedly tell them they're clumsy, fat, dull, or stupid.

One boy whom my daughter dated had a low self-image even though he is handsome and the girls liked him. As a child he was uncoordinated and his family nicknamed him "the klutz." After 18 years as the klutz, he had difficulty imagining he could walk across a room without tripping.

A good friend of mine became depressed each time we went shopping for clothes. One day I asked her why she disliked what for most women is fun. "My mother always took me shopping with my pretty younger sister," she said. "Everything looked good on her and Mother would say, 'It's too bad nothing ever looks right on you. You're just too skinny!" The mother didn't mean to hurt her, but she reinforced a low self-image and programmed this girl for depression.

A charming couple we met while traveling came through our town and stopped by to see us. They had three children with them, and all behaved nicely. During the conversation while the children were in our presence, the mother sighed and said, "I assume you have noticed that Johnny is our problem child." I hadn't, but Johnny surely did.

Some women have a healthy attitude about themselves until they marry a superior being who lets them know what dummies they really are.

Some men run off with their secretaries because they hear nothing but criticism at home. It is amazing how quickly we can destroy one another's self-image by constantly pointing out failures and flaws instead of accenting the positive.

Living in a lovely home with intelligent, even famous,

parents will not guarantee a positive, self-assured child. Often the more outstanding a parent, the more depressed the child becomes—especially if he believes he'll never make it big like his father. What a responsibility we have to make sure our children and our mates do not struggle through defeated, dreary lives! *A low self-image leads to depression.*

10. *Those with too high standards.* Some of us, pushed by either parents or mates, or else driven by our own standards of perfection, set impossible goals for ourselves and become depressed when we cannot make them. I've dealt with many women who determined that their homes would be in museum condition at all times but ended up with themselves and their children in a state of despair.

I used to be a fanatical housekeeper, until one day my husband said, "I wish there was one chair in this house where I felt I could sit down and be comfortable." I began to evaluate the time and anguish I spent on my showplace and decided to lower my standards to a point where we could all relax.

A doctor's wife came to me one day and told me her child was peculiar. She and her husband are neat and their older son is like them. They love the house to be perfect and keep everything in its place. When they read a book they put the book jacket aside so it will always look fresh. The monthly magazines lie untouched on the coffee table in even rows, not to be read until new ones come in to replace them. One day as this lady walked into the living room her young child looked up at her, grabbed a magazine from the table, and ripped it to shreds.

The poor boy wasn't peculiar. He just couldn't stand this perpetual perfection. The standards were unreal and he could no longer play their game.

A psychiatrist who worked with the families of the group of teens who committed suicide in Clear Lake, Texas, told me that the overall reason for the killings seemed to be the youths' inability to achieve what the parents expected of them. Some were the offspring of NASA scientists and all had been brought up with high standards of academic excellence. While there is nothing wrong with high standards, they must be realistic for the individual child, and with the goals must be some loving affirmation of whatever achievement the young person makes.

One suicide note left behind by a Christian teenager said in big print across the top:

> THIS IS REPORT CARD DAY
> I *HATE* REPORT CARD DAY!
>
> I hate to hear "You could have done better."
> Dear God, I hope there are no report cards in heaven. I never want to hear "You could have done better" again.
> Amen.

Dr. Louis Hott, psychiatrist and medical director at the Karen Horney Clinic, says that depressed people come from homes where little love is shown. The individual has "an injured pride and a self-despising image as well as an inability to live up to the demands he feels society makes on him. No matter how much he achieves, it is never up to his standards, because his standards are a glorified image of what *should* be. He feels guilty. Therefore, he is in a constant state of conflict and despair. *Those with unreasonable standards can't help but be depressed.*

11. *Those who feel guilty.* Some of us were programmed from childhood to feel guilty for not getting all A's on our report cards, or for thoughtlessly leaving mother at home alone when we went to a movie. In the humorous book *How to Be a Jewish Mother*, the author tells women that to be successful mothers they must instill such guilt in their children that they will feel duty-bound to support their parents in their old age. Perhaps you've said to your children, "Oh, that's all right. You take the money for a new coat and I'll just shiver in my sweater." "You just eat all the tasty chicken; I'll be glad to have a plain old peanut butter sandwich."

One day as I rushed from a women's club meeting to pick up my Lauren from high school, I was muttering about how overworked I was. She looked at me and said, "It would really be nice, Mother, if you could come just once without pointing out what a sacrifice you had to make to pick me up." I hadn't realized I had become a "Jewish mother."

In my study on incest and child abuse for my book *Lives on the Mend*, I found from each case history that the molested child grows up feeling that he or she is indeed responsible for the act. Even though any objective person can see differently, the victim bears a burden of guilt that is almost impossible for him to shed.

"Incest is a whole question of power, control, betrayal, and deceit going on within a family," comments Joyce N. Thomas, director of the child protective unit of the National Hospital Medical Center in Washington, D. C. It is a crime that by its very nature almost always occurs in the privacy of the home without witnesses—and when revealed often pits the word of a child against that of an adult, a situation in which the child is often the loser. Frequently the child who is a victim of incest feels not only guilt about what has been occurring between her and an adult male but also responsibility. She feels that she has somehow "caused" the sexual abuse and knows that a likely consequence of revealing what is going on will cause the breakup of her already troubled family.[6]

Jan Frank, my prime example on incest, shares how she felt so guilty for what had been done to her by her stepfather that she assumed the guilt for everything that went wrong in her life. "If it rained, I somehow felt it was my fault."

I have learned that women who have been victimized apologize profusely for trivial incidents. If I brush up against a lady in a crowd and she immediately says something like, "I'm so sorry, please forgive me," I can assume she is carrying a load of guilt from the past.

This heavy burden of responsibility for another person's abusive behavior brings with it a terrifying toll on the emotions of the victim.

Those who carry deep guilt feelings, for whatever reason, easily become depressed. *Hovering guilt clouds settle into depression.*

Others who tend to depression and/or suicide are:

Those who have already attempted suicide.
Those who have relatives or friends who are suicidal or have taken their lives.
Those who have emotional disorders (schizophrenics, manic-depressives, neurotics, etc.).
Those who are alcoholics or drug-abusers.

Those with compulsive behavior (gambling, overeating, shoplifting, etc.).

Those teens who are insecure, lonely, and in emotional turmoil.

Those people who don't eat correctly, live on junk food, have hormone imbalances, or suffer from PMS.

Those who are Vietnam veterans and feel disgraced and discredited.

Those women who are trying to balance high-stress professions with family responsibilities.

Those who are lonely and feel abandoned, especially elderly men.

Those who have been victimized in any way and know that life isn't fair.

5

How to Blow Away
the Black Cloud

If you have been going steady with your little black cloud for very long, you may be sick of gloomy days. You may view your depression as hopeless. You may want to ignore the symptoms or rationalize around them, but when you are willing to face depression squarely, the results can be positive. Dr. Frederic Flach in his book *The Secret Strength of Depression* says, "Depression can give many people a unique opportunity. It may be their chance to redefine themselves and to resolve long-standing destructive conflicts within themselves."[1]

Where do we start?

1. *Recognize the problem.* Whether you are bored, lonely, and discouraged or else exhausted, overwhelmed, and suicidal, the first step toward recovery is to face the fact that you have a problem. When I first started dealing with troubled people, I assumed that everyone wanted an answer. My approach was pragmatic: Here's your problem; here's your answer; now get on with it. While this worked for some people, I

soon found that many people wouldn't admit they had a problem. It was someone else's fault and there was nothing they could do about it.

Earlier I mentioned a woman named Gertrude who was depressed because her husband had left her. She was shapeless, sloppily dressed, and dirty, but felt the problem was with her husband. He was the bad guy. As I talked with her and asked what she could have done differently, she replied, "I have been a good wife. He's the one who is running around." It's always difficult to shift the perspective in a case like this because it's so easy to blame the one who left.

"Did your husband ever comment on your physical appearance?" I asked Gertrude hesitantly.

"Oh, yes! He was always looking at other women and telling me I should dress up like them, but I didn't pay any attention to that. If he were really spiritual, he would love me just as I am."

With an answer like that, where was I to go? She was depressed, yet refused to believe she might be any part of her problem marriage. She was determined to sit there chubby with her own black cloud and wait for her husband to become spiritual and return.

The best solutions in the world won't help a person who is unwilling to admit he has a need. When it's the other people's fault, what is there to do but sit in misery and wait for the villains to improve? An extremely angry man came up to me one evening and yelled, "I am furious at my whole family! I wouldn't get upset if they would just do things right! I've made it all so clear!" Putting the blame on others relieves us of having to take any curative action ourselves.

To face the reality of our situation, we don't have to put on a T-shirt that says "I'm depressed" or carry a big sign saying, "Stop the world—I want to get off."

But we have to admit that we have a problem and know that we must do something about it. In an article titled, "If 1977 was LOUSY," Jane O'Reilly writes, "Going back to bed is a sure cure for a bad day, and it sometimes works for a bad week. But when it begins to look like a long haul, going back to bed eventually becomes boring, and worse, it becomes depressing. Besides, if you are in bed, you may not realize it is safe to get up again.

"So get out of bed and try to reconcile yourself to a no-good year. At least now you know you can stop beating your head against the wall."

So get out of bed and realize there is work to be done.

Question 1: Do you recognize that you have a problem?

2. *Decide that you need help.* Some people actually enjoy being miserable and wouldn't accept a good answer if one were handed to them. Psychologist Gary Frieden of the University of Southern California concluded after testing students with low self-esteem, "When feeling bad about themselves, people actively choose to suffer."

In my own counseling I've discovered that many women don't want help even though they've asked for it. Some women with a low self-image merely want a counselor to agree that their situation is hopeless and put the stamp of approval on a life of martyred misery.

Judy came to me at a women's retreat. She was an attractive blond of 35, stylishly dressed but enveloped by a resident black cloud. As she dropped into the chair across from me, I sank lower in mine. Judy was obviously depressed, yet as she told me her story she seemed to enjoy reliving her past. The more miserable the message, the brighter her narrative. She had obviously told the tale many times and seemed to take pride in her history of suffering. Her first husband had been handsome, hardworking, faithful, and frugal, and had plans for the future. Judy didn't like the time Neal spent at work and resented his apparent indifference to her physical ailments. "I was always sickly and my parents really cared. Neal's mother was healthy as an ox and she told him my sickness was all in my head."

Judy had learned as a child that constant colds brought consistent attention, but Neal let her suffer alone, and this was no fun. As he overlooked her complaints, she sank into more drastic ailments and assorted surgeries. Eventually Neal tired of a "sickly" wife and went off with a gym teacher who could run all day without even an aspirin.

After the divorce Judy perked up long enough to win Frank, a friend of Neal's who dropped by to console her. "I was lonesome and needed a shoulder to cry on," she explained to me. "Frank was always there, and one day he asked me to marry him. 'Why not?' I thought. 'I have nothing better to do.' So we picked up two friends and went to a Justice of the Peace. As I heard him recite the vows I said to myself, 'What are you doing here getting married to a man you don't even love?' I knew right then that it was wrong."

As Judy told me of this mistake that lasted only four months, she seemed to find pleasure in her miseries, but the best was yet to come. The recounting of her third marriage made her close to euphoric. Jonathan was a charming and seductive con artist who literally swept her off her feet and into his apartment. "From the moment I laid eyes on him, I fell madly in love." Judy had no time to be sickly because she had to support Jonathan. He was too handsome to work, so she held down two jobs to keep him in Gucci shoes and a yellow Porsche. Judy never asked him where he spent his time and even accepted a nine-year-old boy that Jonathan moved in one night. "He told me the child was his by some former friend, and he knew I would take him as my own." Judy juggled work and motherhood while Jonathan played. One day she came home to find the child gone and a note from Jonathan's "friend" which said, "I took him back, you bum!"

At this point, Judy confessed, she began to have doubts about her marriage, but she didn't have to wonder long, for the following week she found Jonathan dead in the bathtub from a drug overdose.

Judy had established a lifetime pattern of sickness and suffering, and my job was to show her a new and positive direction. "Do you want help, or are you happy in your miseries?" I asked bluntly. She wasn't really sure.

Until a person wants help, there's no point in outlining a solution.

Question 2: Do you really want help, or do you choose to suffer?

3. *Examine the causes.* In order to lift our black cloud, we must positively and honestly examine the reasons for our depression. What is it that gets me down? Is the family room always cluttered? The sink always full of dishes? The laundry always overflowing the hamper?

At one point in my life I was overwhelmed with housework. Then I examined the problem and decided I hadn't properly utilized my family's manpower. Inwardly I wanted to do the work myself. This way I could complain that I was overworked and under-appreciated! I was, in effect, becoming a martyr mother. But then I changed. With my husband's help I scheduled the basic chores, divided the house into areas, wrote down the duties for each section, and made a work chart assigning each child his jobs. I trained them for their responsibilities, put the chart where all could see it, and turned the bulk of the housework over to them. At that point I had two of my own children at home and two young adults living with us as part of the family. Now I am able to travel, knowing that my 22-year-old son will keep the house in order.

Those of you with little children may feel your house will always be a mess. I had one friend who believed this was true and gave up. She put the playpen in the living room, filled it with lamps, figurines, and other breakables, and then let the children run wild through the house. It was a depressing home to visit.

Children must be taught to respect property and pick up their things, but they will only learn as we continually work with them. Train them and praise them for their help and for a job well done, and soon they'll be helping you.

For you discouraged mothers, try to have at least one room in the house where the children don't go. It could be the living room, the study, or a spare bedroom. Keep it in good order and rest in the assurance that if a friend drops by you will have one neat place where you can sit down and share a cup of tea.

Sometimes the cloud that hangs over our head is job-related. A lady once called to tell me she had heard me speak at a FEMINAR and for the first time realized that her fatigue and indifference to life were signs of depression. She began to wonder what the cause of her discontentment was and suddenly realized she disliked teaching school. She never thought of leaving her profession, yet when she understood her constant gloom was because she didn't like her job, she began thinking of alternatives. She reviewed what she enjoyed doing and became excited when she thought of her hobby—collecting antiques. One afternoon she approached a friend in the antique business who was looking for an intelligent associate and he hired her immediately. The woman called to tell me she had examined the cause and had taken action. Now she starts each day with enthusiasm—her depression is gone. She concluded by saying, "Thank you for making me recognize I had a problem and encouraging me to do something about it."

One lady wrote to tell me she had tried tracing her depression and found that it stemmed from a conflict with a friend. Some unkind things had passed between them, and later she found that her facts were wrong. She had avoided her friend and thought the matter was out of her mind. When she began to trace the cause of her gloomy feelings, she realized she felt guilty over her unpleasant behavior. She forced herself to go to her friend's home and apologize. "It wasn't easy," she wrote, "but after we had cried together, our relationship was restored and we are friends again. Thank you for making me seek the reason for my depression."

In a mild depression these simple steps may be all it takes.

Question 3: What are you depressed about today?

4. *Look at the alternatives.* When we face depression openly, it will usually improve. After you bring it to the surface, seek help from a friend or counselor. At this point it is helpful to look realistically at the alternatives. What possible answers are available?

Dana poured out her problems one night at a group session of a women's conference. I had seen her each year at this event as a leader, but that night she became a case. Her husband of 22 years had left her for a younger woman. She pleaded with him to give her another chance, wrote him love letters, and begged him to take her out to dinner each week. But her pleas brought no positive results. He told her the more she cried the less he ever wanted to see her again. She was humiliated among her peers and wanted to die.

As she shared her story, four others in the group admitted that they were in similar situations, and we began to look at the human alternatives.

1. Stay miserable and depressed. (That was where they all were hovering. They didn't realize there was any other choice.)
2. Run away from home. (They all smiled at this alternative because escape was the only pleasant possibility to rescue them from embarrassment and loneliness.)
3. Accept the fact that he's gone and get on with a new life.

Point three was an unpopular but realistic choice. Accept the fact that he's gone. The five dejected girls agreed that they had worked hard to avoid accepting an unacceptable situation. They had all played various games with themselves, had pretended they were in a bad dream, and had concentrated intensely on wishing him home again, but nothing had worked and they were depressed.

"Accepting that he's gone does not preclude his ever coming back," I said. "In fact, it may hasten his return."

An errant husband once told me, "Once she stopped sniveling and pleading and got herself pulled together, I could see there was hope and I came back."

Dana chose the third alternative. She accepted her husband's absence and analyzed her potential. She admitted that she was overweight, went on an effective diet, had her hair styled, and exchanged her old method of makeup for a fresh and natural look. She bought a few well-chosen clothes and began to look for a job. Much to her surprise, she was hired as a TV weathergirl and life looked hopeful again.

One beautiful and stylish friend of mine was shocked when she overheard her Christian husband on the phone professing love to another woman. She confronted him and he admitted he was having an affair. He said he loved them both, and in her attempts to win him back she went along with his threesome arrangement, going out to dinner together and even cooking for the other woman. She wanted to make sure she had done all that God would expect of her and even more. In spite of her patient acceptance of this husband's bizarre behavior, the day came when this man told her to leave. After a year of devout prayer, hours of daily Bible study, and unmatched personal purity, she had been unable to change his mind. She grieved for what should have been and asked God to show her what she could do. There were no answers—only the draining of her strength and energy.

One night I suggested that we have a funeral for the man and bury him for good. This would definitely not be a first step in solving marriage problems, but at the end of a long line of rebuffs, insults, degradation, and divorce papers, it seemed the only way to save her sanity. We knelt by the coffee table and asked God to remove the unresolved guilt she was carrying and the daily nagging reminders of a marriage that once was and to put it all to rest.

Later she told me that our funeral was a turning point. She stopped pleading for a return of the past, faced the reality of this shocking choice that her husband had made, and began to set new goals for her unwanted single life.

We in the Christian community would like to avoid admitting we have problems like divorce, but we must face the reality of the times and realize that the divorced person is depressed to some degree at least some of the time and needs our encouragement and prayerful support.

Eating disorders and depression go hand-in-hand. As children we received ice cream and candy as rewards, and so when we're depressed we reward ourselves with treats. In many churches the social life revolves around food. I spend much of my time at lunches, brunches, and banquets. Before I was 50 I thought all overweight women had no self-discipline, but now I have to examine my own choices more closely. Whatever the reason for overeating, the depressed chubby lady must look at her alternatives.

1. Stay heavy and depressed over her size-44 dress.
2. Talk about diets and read books on reducing.
3. Accept herself as she is and stop focusing on her size.
4. Admit she has a problem and get on with some realistic program for steady weight loss, improved nutrition, and exercise.

To those who are not overweight, the choice looks simple, but to those of us who have been struggling with this problem for years, a change seems frightening or even impossible.

In a seminar Emilie Barnes was speaking on diet. She told of her "fat friend" who would bake a cake for her family and not eat any herself. But the following morning, after everyone left, she would wolf down the remaining cake. In order to cover up her gluttony, she would bake an identical cake, eat half of that, and present the leftover cake for dessert on a second night. By the time she willingly faced her alternatives, she was so immense that she was placed in a reducing sanatorium for a month of deprogramming.

Sometime after sharing this story Emilie received a letter from Lauri, one of the participants. Lauri wrote that she had been offended at Emilie's use of the phrase "fat friend." Lauri had known she was overweight but never thought of herself as *fat*. But as she sat around eating potato chips and thinking about Emilie's story, it struck her that maybe she *was* fat. The more she thought about it, the more convicted she became that indeed she was fat. Lauri took out the material on diet and studied it. By the time Lauri wrote the letter, she had lost 30 pounds and thanked Emilie for using the word *fat*. "Overweight never got to me," she said, "but I really didn't want to be *fat*!

So many fat people try to consider themselves pleasingly plump and rationalize that all chubby people are jolly. But they're not. They are often depressed, and while they may try to laugh a lot in public, they often weep at home when the zipper just won't make it.

The easiest alternative is to stay fat. It takes no effort, and diets don't work anyway.

The next alternative is a clever cover-up. The overweight person talks about diets and eats only salads when out with friends. She explains that her problem is glandular, "but you can see I'm trying." She reads each new book on weight reduction and will freely recite the difference between Dr. Stillman and Dr. Atkins.

I stayed in the home of one plump lady who had a beautiful face but too much beneath it. She ate very little the first night and chronicled a lengthy list of futile diets she had tried. Scattered around the coffee tables were assortments of diet books which she picked up and read whenever she sat down. Her life was absorbed with the study of weight reduction, yet she hadn't lost an ounce. Every time she mentioned diet, her children would sigh, shake their heads, and look the other way. One daughter told me, "We don't mind her being fat if she'd only shut up about it."

She pushed me to give her advice, and after a few questions I discovered her underlying problems. Her husband was a traveling salesman and she was angry that he had "all the fun" while she stayed home. She ate to punish him. When I pointed this out, she vehemently rejected my analysis, but after some soul-searching she admitted, "I guess I've been trying to get even with him and the reading is just a cover-up."

She joined Weight Watchers, studied their material, and put the program into practice.

The third choice is to accept the size you are and stop worrying about it. Stay neat and attractive and wear clothes that fit and are not gaping between buttons. One heavy friend of mine always looks sensational and models professionally. The audience always applauds her because she is realistic and they can relate to her. Besides, those anorexic models make us all feel guilty.

The fourth alternative is to face the problem and get on with it. Stormie Omartian's book *Greater Health God's Way* clearly outlines the steps we need to take to be healthy and fit. One day after I had been following her plan for about a month and had lost only a few pounds, I asked her what I was doing wrong. She replied, "Are you doing *everything* I say?"

"Well, close to it," I answered.

"Are you exercising?"

That was the fatal question.

I bought her tape and began to exercise. When I do it faithfully I lose, and when I can't find the time I gain.

There are many health plans available to us, but they only work in proportion to our dedication and consistency.

Betty Wright from Riverside sent me these personal thoughts after hearing me speak on depression:

> Some of us have never learned to think. We act on raw emotion and selfish desires. My suggestion is for a person to sum up his problem in one short sentence. Next write down all the solutions and make a decision. Indecisiveness only adds to one's anxiety and nervousness.
>
> We can save ourselves much anxiety and frustration by defining our problems. For example, I bought a convertible bed, but when it was delivered, it didn't appear to be the item I had chosen. I could choose to gripe, complain, bad-mouth the store, and get depressed, or I could simply write down the solutions and choose one. My alternatives were 1) return it and choose another, 2) get my money back, or 3) not complain and keep it because I needed it and didn't have time to shop for another. I chose and accepted the third alternative.

We have to decide whether we want to choose the most sensible alternative in our situation. The other alternative is to get emotional, gripe, or give the attitude that the world is against us.

If you are depressed and feel you need a new direction, make a list of your alternatives. Be willing to think courageously and creatively. Don't accept the status quo. Be willing for a new vitality to break in on your life.

Question 4: What are your alternatives? Write them down.

1) _____
2) _____
3) _____

Cross out any that do not appear to be sensible choices. Concentrate on a hopeful answer to your problems.

5. *Check your health.* Sometimes depression is caused by some body misfunction. Several years ago I sank into a period of unexplainable exhaustion and could hardly move. When I had to speak I would "psych myself up" and force myself to go, but when it was over I would collapse for hours. Several doctors gave me alternatives: It was either all in my head, a bored housewife syndrome, or a bid for attention. I knew these diagnoses weren't true and persisted until I found a doctor who gave me a five-hour glucose tolerance test. The results showed I had severe hypoglycemia. My adrenal glands functioned only on high or zero and my blood sugar was extremely low. With a high-protein diet, raw fruits and vegetables, vitamins and minerals, *and absolutely no sugar*, I returned to normal. Each time I share this experience with women, I find at least one in a similar condition.

Not every doctor can spot hypoglycemia and some will tell you, "There is no such thing."

Earlier I mentioned Jane. One day she came up to

me at a retreat: overweight, lacking in style, sloppily dressed, and exhausted. She told me she was unable to keep up with her basic housework and just wanted to stay in bed all day. Her husband had sent her to the retreat hoping the change would do her good. I suggested that she find a doctor who could recognize hypoglycemia and have an exam. Later she wrote, "My tests showed I have extremely low blood sugar. I'm already feeling better on my new diet."

Researchers have found definite connections between low blood sugar and depression. California State Senator Robert Presley introduced a bill calling for a state study of hypoglycemia, an illness which he said is related to antisocial behavior. The measure would require the Department of Health to study juvenile offenders who suffer from the disease to see if there is a connection between the sugar problem and criminal tendencies.

Other physical problems can also lead to depression: a misfunction of the endocrine glands, hypothyroidism, and hormone imbalance during menopause. If you can't find an obvious reason for your depression, check your health.

Don't be discouraged if the first doctor doesn't locate your problem. Doris Ryen, a counselor at Moorhead State University in Minnesota, interviewed 96 hypoglycemics and found, "Forty-five percent had seen three or more doctors before being diagnosed. Fifteen percent had seen from six to fifteen doctors before hypoglycemia was diagnosed, and seventeen people mentioned that they themselves requested the doctor give them the glucose tolerance test. Furthermore, almost half felt they had hypoglycemia five years or more before being diagnosed."

With the new interest in health foods, vitamins, and

exercise, Americans are conscious of how important it is to care for their bodies. More and more people are aware of the harmful effects of sugar; even teenagers are willing to admit that a steady diet of Cokes and potato chips is dangerous.

In a medical digest from the Gannett News Service I read:

> If you're a coffee drinker and feeling unusually depressed, you might try doing without for a while just to see if you feel better. That's suggested by an experiment involving eighty-three psychiatric patients at a veteran's hospital.
>
> Researchers there found that the higher the intake of caffeine from all sources (coffee, tea, cola, drinks and medicines containing caffeine), the more likely it was for the patients to suffer from increased depression and anxiety.

According to the American Health Education Foundation, the lack of B vitamins can cause a depressed state of mind. They claim that nutritionally oriented physicians are having dramatic results with an "anti-depression megavitamin regimen" which includes large amounts of vitamin B-1, niacinamide, niacin, pantothenic acid, vitamin C, magnesium, and minerals. For further information on this program, write the American Health Education Foundation, 693 Main Street, Hackensack, New Jersey 07601.

Glamour magazine ran a page called "Foods to help you cope with moods." Under "Food and Depression" they instructed us to stay away from salty foods, sugar, fatty foods, and heavy meals. "*Sweets* boost your spirits for a while, but in a short time you're spiraling down again. And for some people, a sugar overload spurs a hypoglycemic reaction and deeper depression." They suggest a warm glass of milk to soothe nerves and tell us to be sure to take our B vitamins. "It's the nerve vitamin—not that one food will cure depression, but according to Philadelphia physician J. H. Feingold, a balanced diet rich in B vitamin foods can, in many cases, pull you through a rocky period without the need of tranquilizers."

A novel approach came out in *The Los Angeles Times* on May 9, 1978. "Running is the newest treatment for depression." Dr. John H. Greist of the University of Wisconsin compared patients who were treated with "running therapy" versus psychotherapy and found that those who ran improved faster. He doesn't know exactly why running has an antidepressant effect but gave some possibilities. "First, it provides an experience of mastery. . . they demonstrated to themselves a capacity for change—they lost weight, reduced their smoking, toned up muscles, changed their body image and felt better about themselves . . . some consciously substituted this positive habit—running—for more negative habits or addictions. They began to feel less angry and anxious."

Is it possible that your depression is related to a physical problem? Do you eat too much sugar? Do you pour salt on greasy French fries? Have you had a complete physical lately? Are you drinking too much coffee? Are you taking your vitamins? Do you exercise every day? Perhaps we can *run away* from our little black cloud!

Question 5: Have you checked your health and physical condition?

6. *Analyze self-pity.* Dr. Tim LaHaye says in his book

The Spirit-Controlled Temperament, "A person becomes depressed only after a period of indulging in the sin of self-pity." Do you feel sorry for yourself? Do you wish you had married the other man that asked you? Or are you still depressed that only one man asked you? Have your children failed to measure up to your standards? Did they forget to send you a card on Mother's Day? Did you get bypassed for a promotion? Do your neighbors hardly know you're alive? Life's problems can totally overwhelm us if we allow self-pity to take hold.

When I first moved to California, I was lonely and felt sorry for myself. I had left a 12-room modern house to move into a shabby old five-room bungalow. I had left a town where everyone knew me for a city where no one cared. Fred and I had left a profitable business to work full-time without pay for a Christian organization. Wasn't I justified in feeling sorry for myself? I surely was. Since then I've learned that *justified depression* is the worst type to overcome. When we can prove that "anyone would be depressed in my circumstances," there is little impetus to improve. I was so homesick that I wrote letters saying how I missed everyone, called home as often as I dared, and saved money to fly back. Then one day I read Philippians 4:11: "I have learned in whatever state I am to be content" (NKJV). Did that mean I was to be happy in the state of California? I concluded I was. The verse convicted me to stop feeling sorry for myself and to make the best of my new state. I got to work on remodeling the old bungalow, joined some clubs, met new friends, and threw away my self-pity. Are you feeling sorry for yourself?

Debbie was depressed. Her husband had made her move again. As I talked to her, I learned that her husband was an aggressive executive in a large company and that they, not he, decided when he was to move. He was always excited about his promotions, but she wanted to settle down. "I don't ask for much," she moaned. "I was happy with the little place we had five houses back."

When I asked if she had really been happy five houses back, she wasn't sure, but she knew she was miserable now. She was living in a big house with a big car and a big boat but seemed to be happy only with the past. I told her I knew at least five women in her town who would get over their own depressions immediately if they could sit in her house, drive in her car, and sail in her boat.

Maturity comes when we are able to accept our present position in life and adjust to our situation with gratitude. We need to praise the Lord anyhow!

Question 6: Are you drowning in self-pity?

7. *Avoid trouble.* If you are a person who is easily influenced by your surroundings, it's especially important that you don't go to depressing places or sit around with gloomy people when you're not in a strong positive mood yourself. This statement seems too obvious to be mentioned; however, I frequently talk with depressed women who have come close to suicide over a morbid movie or a mournful friend. While we can't spend our lives avoiding problems, we can stay away from overbearing circumstances when we are already unhappy.

If you get easily depressed, don't visit the friend who catalogs her ailments or marital difficulties through lunch. Two sad souls make a miserable group. Don't choose your worst moments to discuss overdue bills with your husband. Don't visit your son's teacher on a day when you can't stand one more negative word.

I once went to a PTA meeting when I was in a good humor only to be devastated by a math teacher. "I am Marita Littauer's mother," I said happily. His one-word answer, "Oh," was said with such a foreboding tone that I knew I was in for trouble.

"How is she doing?" I dared to ask.

"Just fine, when she comes."

When I learned that my adorable child was cutting math because it interfered with lunch, it turned my cheerfulness into a feeling of humiliation and hopelessness. From that experience I learned to evaluate possibilities and take on the worst when I felt the best. When we think preventively, we can save ourselves unnecessary grief.

Some depressed women are like vacuum cleaners: They suction up bad news all day and then empty it all out on the family at dinner. One man told me, "I don't know how she comes up with those hard-luck stories, but the last thing I need to hear each night is the dreary tales of all the misfits she's found."

When you're in a low mood, don't spend the day reviewing your burdens. Visit a cheerful friend! Go out to lunch at a special restaurant or go shopping at a different store. Look at the latest fashions. If you are trying to avoid trouble, don't watch the sex, suffering, and sin on the afternoon soap operas. Take your mind off the negatives and accentuate the positive.

One Saturday I spoke to 250 teenagers, members of a high-class society league. When I asked for examples of how they helped their mothers, one bright girl called out, "I try to cheer my mother up when the people on her soap operas have a bad day. When Lee Randolf committed suicide, she cried for hours."

I assumed this was an isolated situation but noticed that a serious mood spread through the group. "How many girls have mothers who are so involved in soap operas that it affects their personalities?'' I asked. Over half the girls raised their hands.

Twenty million Americans watch the soaps, and on any given afternoon you can entertain in your own home:

> . . .a weeping woman in the throes of a bitter divorce.

> . . .a mournful adolescent who somehow got pregnant through no fault of her own.

> . . .a dashing doctor who devastates nurses in the linen closet while his wife dies slowly in the next room.

> . . .a pair of drug addicts who would beat up their own mothers for a fix.

> . . .a few liberated youths who feel that living together is the next best thing.

> . . .a penitent politician producing novels in prison while awaiting parole.

> . . .an absurd alcoholic who once was a bank president and is now collecting shells.

> . . .and a pitiful lady with amnesia who has forgotten her third husband locked up in the mental hospital after attempted suicide.

Is there any possibility that you could fellowship with these felons and not get depressed?

Question 7: Are you out looking for trouble?

6

Start Blowing

If you have considered the preceding suggestions, you have already made positive strides in the right direction. Now where do you go from here?

1. *Take action.* Shakespeare tells us to take arms against a sea of troubles and, by opposing, end them. Are you ready to take arms?

Dr. Maxwell Maltz in his *Psycho-cybernetics* says, "No one can deny that there is also a perverse sense of satisfaction in feeling sorry for yourself."[1] Indeed, some of us do get so comfortable in our depression that we really don't want to get out of it. The feeling is like wearing a faded blue housecoat for years and years. I once kept one that had even lost a few buttons. It looked awful, but it felt so comfortable. It had become a part of me. Depression, too, can become a part of us; it can wrap us up like an old bathrobe; it can become a way of life.

Hopefully by now you want to take action and find the silver lining in your black cloud.

What are some human steps you can take to get your

thoughts on a positive level?

Since depression is a conviction of one's own help-lessness, one human step to relieve this problem is to find some area where you are proficient. Think for a minute about something in which you have an above-average ability or knowledge. *Do you have musical talent?* Find a local group you can join, even if it means giving up another commitment you feel you "should" be doing.

Do you have leadership ability that your family equates with bossiness? Seek a natural channel to make the best use of these qualities. Many groups limp along because they have no creative leadership. I once became president of the Connecticut Speech and Drama Association on my first meeting before I had even joined.

Are strangers attracted to you and instantly dump their problems on you? Some women have a gift for counseling and don't realize the need there is in social agencies, hotlines, and churches for an encouraging word from a good listener. I find myself giving advice in supermarket lines and often counsel strangers in ladies' rooms.

The prime need we all have in time of depression is a feeling of self-worth. What can you do to lift your value in your own eyes? What thought comes to your mind right now? How can you put this idea into practice? Make a goal using your talent and/or desires, then write down steps to achieve this goal. Don't be discouraged when the path looks too difficult. Accept this as part of the challenge. Remember: No goal = no achievement = depression.

Joan Kennedy wrote in *McCall's*:

> In times of crisis and expectation, I could rise to the occasion and not take a drink. But

then the show is over and you are left with
no goal to go back to, and you feel desperately let down and unneeded.

Become involved in projects that fit your abilities,
and don't listen to those who tell you, "It's impossible."
Reaching the goal is not as important, at this point, as
having one.

Sue came to one of our FEMINARS. She was seeking
something to brighten up her life. Before her marriage
she had been a home economics teacher, but as she
assessed her abilities she became discouraged—they
seemed so ordinary. She felt all she could do with pro-
ficiency was cook and bake bread. As she listened to
our section on diet and nutrition, she realized she
wasn't feeding her family properly. She set a goal to
study all she could about good nutrition, bought a
wheat mill and mixer, and installed a water distiller. Her
neighbors became interested and soon she was demon-
strating her equipment. She became a distributor for
the mill, mixer, and distiller, began to speak to women's
groups, and now teaches cooking on TV. She and her
husband, Rich, started their own Nutrition Seminars
followed by personal consultation and menu-planning.
All this because Sue was willing to expand her sights!

What are your interests, abilities, or desires? Find
them. Set a reasonable goal. Study, read, practice—
whatever it takes to give you a feeling of accomplishment. Remember: Indecision is a close brother to
depression. Start to move today! Force yourself right
now to examine your prospects and make a plan.

Do not fear failure. I have failed at tennis, archery,
painting, and piano, but I have had modest gains in
cooking, writing, speaking, and crewel embroidery. If
you don't enter any races, you can never be a winner.

Question 1: Are you ready to get moving? Write down at least one new goal that you would enjoy achieving.

---

2. *Get organized.* Some of you are probably saying, "If she only knew how much I have to do, she wouldn't be suggesting that I try something new." Obviously the old routine has not excited you, so why not try some new trick? Perhaps you are weighted down with housework. Do you have to be? Remember the adage that work expands to fit the time available. If you've got all day to do your chores, it will take longer. If you have to be out of the house by 9:00, you will make it.

My adopted son, Fred, once returned from a vacation with a family who have "The White Glove Lady" come in each day and do the housework. He was fascinated and wanted to bring her home. Unfortunately, I am my own White Glove Lady, and Fred and Marita are gray glove helpers. You may have some little gloves around the house that you have not yet put to work. I find that most depressed women make martyrdom a virtue. They would rather die dusting than teach a child how to lift a finger. I now run an opposite course. I have trained the troops.

To spend as little time as possible on housework, you have to get organized. You need to list what has to be done, assign the tasks to available bodies, and then see that the chores are done. I started young Fred on housework as soon as he could stand up. I showed him how to carry hampers to the laundry room. He then learned how to dump them out. This was such fun that he sometimes filled them up again just to dump them.

Once he had these tasks under control, I showed him how to sort the laundry. Later he learned how to operate the washing machine, use the dryer, and fold clothes. When I am away, he runs the house. When I return, the house is in order and there is always a fresh cloth on the table and clean towels in the bathroom. Don't wait until your child is 14 to start training him to work. Make it an early habit, and expected part of life.

I make use of every set of hands. When Fred was in fifth grade a little boy came to spend a night with him. He enjoyed himself and stayed for a week. On the third day I put his name on the work chart and assigned him jobs. I overheard him tell Fred, "Your mother must really like me. She put my name on the family work chart." When children are shown what to do and are praised for their accomplishments, they become eager helpers.

Aside from making use of available glovepower, what else can you do to get organized? Perhaps you are depressed because you've never finished the housework. Nothing has ever been perfect. I've been married 33 years and have never risen clearly above the waters, but with organization, the swimming is easier.

Let's pretend your house is a mess right now and you know it's hopeless. What a great basis for eternal depression! Why not set a reasonable goal? Clean one room a day for as long as you have rooms. Write this schedule down and then start. Just seeing in print that you will have a clean house a week from Tuesday will lift your spirits.

Start with the kitchen. Take everything out one cabinet at a time. Put all the odd glasses and jelly jars in a box for the church rummage sale and buy some matching ones at K-Mart. Put covers on all the refrigerator jars and then throw out the jars and covers that have no mates. This act alone will give you an empty shelf. Stuff all the odd plastic plates and spoons into a box labeled ''Good for Picnics''—in case you ever have one—and put it in the garage. Throw out the torn placemats and turn the faded tablecloths into dusters. Check your canned goods and give away the six cans of artichoke hearts you bought on sale and are afraid to serve your family. Give your neighbor the big bag of dog food you bought the week before Spot died. Do you get the idea? By the time you finish the kitchen, you will be deliriously happy and ready to tackle your bedroom closet in the morning. What a productive way to overcome depression!

After you have organized each room and clearly labeled your shelves, explain to the family that you need their cooperation to keep the house in order. Tell them this isn't just a passing phase, then make sure it isn't. For further help in household organization and practical steps you can take to get out from under your piles of work, read my friend Emilie Barnes' books *More House in My Day* and *Survival for Busy Women*.

Have each family member make his bed before breakfast, and assign one member to see that it's done. Serve one breakfast at one time (versus playing short-order cook) and insist that they all appear.

Jessica, a depressed girl, told me that she started breakfast at 6:30 each morning and was still cooking to order at 8:30 without having a bite herself. I got depressed just thinking of two hours over a hot stove each morning. After our discussion, she got her family up at the same time, served a good balanced breakfast, sat down with them herself, did the dishes, and was done with the whole job in less than an hour. The family enjoyed breakfast together, Jessica no longer dreaded getting up in the morning, and the children had an extra hour to do their chores.

Assign each child to keep his room clean and then define what clean is. Don't nag them into perfection or they will become depressed and run away to live with the sloppy lady down the street.

Set times for them to deliver their wash to the laundry area. If your husband watches television each evening, perhaps you could do laundry then. You can sit dutifully beside him and then run and push a few buttons during commercials. There are few TV shows whose impact will be diluted by the folding of a few towels.

For those of you who have never tried this organized road to ecstasy, perhaps you should put the book down and start cleaning. You may get so happy that you will have no need to finish reading!

Question 2: Are you willing to get organized? List what areas in your life need to be pulled together:

_____   _____

_____   _____

3. *Get your priorities in order.* Now that your house is clean, let's make sure your priorities are in order. While some women spend too much time alone at home, some stay away if at all possible. Their reasons? Boring housework, demanding husbands, and intolerable children. The depressing results of this flight are that the house gets worse, the husband complains more strongly, and the children have tantrums just to get Mother's attention.

Are you so involved in "meaningful activities" that you are neglecting the home front? This was the problem with Lynn. As I listened to her plight, she told me what excited her. She modeled twice a week for a local store, worked part-time selling designer dresses, and was chairman of several committees. Home and family were boring.

Lynn, dressed in a striking Evan-Picone suit, explained, "If I didn't have to go home, I would never be depressed. As long as I'm running around I'm happy, but when I stop at a red light on the way home, a wave of gloom seems to hit me."

My husband and I agreed to go out for dinner with Lynn and John. He was quiet, attractive, and successful, but it was apparent that Lynn found him dull. He supported her well and came home every night, but he wasn't exciting enough for Lynn.

She was fitfully fleeing the reality of a drab marriage and disturbed children. One daughter had been treated by several doctors and sent to a specialist for hyperactive children. All the doctors agreed that the girl needed a calm and stable living situation. John explained that the child was supposed to have a schedule she could count on, and then he said, "But that's impossible. We haven't eaten dinner at the same time twice since we've been married."

They needed to get their priorities in order, yet when I tried to outline a plan Lynn muttered, "It would be so much easier if the doctors could just give the kid some pills to calm her down."

Are you like Lynn? Are you spinning your wheels and getting nothing accomplished? Would you rather take a pill than get your act together? When we run around seeking pleasure and neglecting our families, we begin to feel guilty. Ultimately, the guilt engulfs us and we become depressed.

Although Lynn avoided responsibility and escaped

her boredom through worldly involvement, many women I talk with do the same thing through their churches. But how could a woman who spends all her time in church possibly be wrong? How could a lady who attends four Bible studies a week have her priorities out of line?

A handsome businessman came up to me at a weekend conference. "If I had known this was going to be religious, I wouldn't have come. I've heard all the Bible verses I ever need and then some." After he calmed down, I learned he had a "saintly wife." Alice served on the music committees, taught Bible studies, cooked church suppers, and put tracts in Harry's suitcase, but was never there when he came home from work. She counseled women on the phone all evening, but never got to bed when he did. From his point of view she was a fraud. He had come to our seminar hoping *she* would get straightened out.

When I talked with Alice I found a mournful, pious woman who was feverishly working out her version of God's plan for her life. She was burdened by her worldly husband and had her Bible study groups praying for his soul.

It is hard to disagree with that kind of firm and positive resolve, yet I had to show Alice that her place was at home with her husband. If she wished to counsel others, she should straighten out her relationship with her husband first or she was living a lie. She must stop laying heavy spiritual truths upon the poor man and start loving him. After Alice reluctantly got the message, I called Harry over and gave them each some suggestions to improve their marriage. He was so glad Alice listened that he stayed for the rest of the seminar and thanked me warmly before he left.

No matter how positive or saintly our activities may

be, we must make sure we have our priorities in order. Let's not "lose" our families while "saving" others!

Question 3: Are your priorities really in order? List what changes you should make.

_____

_____

4. *Improve yourself.* In her book *How to Say YES to Life: A Woman's Guide to Beating the Blahs*, Catherine Miller makes suggestions to the depressed middle-aged woman who is suffering from the empty-nest syndrome. "She may have to begin with her physical appearance, to build her self-confidence. It may sound superficial to worry about hair, nails, skin, and figure, but if you're a woman who looks in the mirror and says, 'I'm too old, I'm too gray-haired, I'm too fat,' then you'll go right back to bed and pull the covers over your head."

Some of us after looking in the mirror and seeing the lines of time etched around our eyes do try to hide from our black clouds by pulling the covers over our heads. For example, in 1978, within two months I had to face the stark reality of middle age. I became a grandmother, had my 25th wedding anniversary, and reached the golden age of 50! Such a combination of events could be discouraging, but my family made it all fun. My mother—bright, slim, and attractive at 80—came out to greet her first great-grandchild and I was uplifted to see how beautifully she carried her age. My daughters planned a gala 25th anniversary party and registered me as a bride at the local department store, and my friends gave me a fresh start with ten place settings of new china. For my birthday my husband took me to the beach for a long weekend and told me I was in better shape than most of the visions on the shore.

While all this family encouragement was reassuring, I decided to evaluate myself physically. I have always felt every woman should do the very best she can with herself. (My husband feels I have done more than could be expected with the raw material available!) I looked at myself and realized that too much of my weight had settled in my hips, so my two daughters and I enrolled in an exercise program at a figure salon. I have never liked anything athletic, but I forced myself to get enthused and walk to the salon each morning at 8:00. If there is anyone who has no time for such a program, I am the one. But I learned to quickly clean up after breakfast, make the bed, apply my makeup, slip into my leotards, and stride with Marita to the salon. After exercising, I would walk home, get dressed, and arrive at my office invigorated by 9:00. I lost several pounds in four months and a few inches in the right places, but more important, I set a goal for improvement and achieved it.

Where do you need help? Is your *weight* holding you home on the couch? Go on a diet, have a contest with a friend, reevaluate your eating habits. Do you have weak arms and flabby legs? If you do, exercise with some slim thing on TV until you look like her. Have some friends in to sway with you or take a dance class at the Y. Having others with you makes even sit-ups seem fun. Also watch for bargain rates at a salon. (We got six months for 25 dollars.) Aerobics are so popular right now that you can find a group just about anywhere. Leotards are available in all colors, and if you're really into dancing, you can add leg-warmers.

Is your *hair* limp and lifeless? No woman ever looks or feels good with dull hair. The TV ads tell you that certain shampoos will double the bulk of your hair and increase its length with one application, but I've never seen such miracles happen. It takes time, effort, and a good hairdresser to brighten your hair, but it's worth the trouble. With enough work your hair may bounce and swing like that of the girls on TV.

Does your *face* draw a blank when you look in the mirror? Has your cheerleader image faded? Is your *makeup* outdated? Do you have circles under your eyes? If you need help but don't know where to go, head for a large department store and ask for a make-over at their cosmetic counter. Look in your phone book for beauty consultants. Ask your hairdresser for help. Read the book Marita and I wrote together called *Shades of Beauty*. This will help you get a feel for what colors will do the most for you and will show you how to apply your makeup. Do whatever suits you, but don't spend another day with your drab face if it's depressing you.

Do you have a closet full of clothes and *nothing to wear*? Pull out all your outfits and examine them. Whatever you haven't worn in two years put in a box labeled "Not good enough to wear but too good to throw away." Match up your skirts and blouses, slacks and sweaters. Do you have a skirt with no top? A sweater that doesn't go with anything? While everything is out, check each item to make sure it's clean and has all its buttons. Don't return anything to the closet that isn't ready to wear and in season. This act of organization will encourage you and give you the assurance that the next time you reach for your clothes they will be fresh and attractive.

In *Shades of Beauty* we show you how to clean out your closet and coordinate your clothing. For eight years Marita has been a cosmetic and color consultant and has done personal color palettes for women. By taking the shades from your hair, the base color and glints from your eyes, and the tone of your skin, she lays out an individual palette suited only to you, guaranteed to enhance your looks if used correctly. Marita didn't choose this career to help depressed women, but we've been amazed how a woman's personalized color chart can lift her confidence and self-image. Somehow knowing that what you're wearing is right for you does lift your spirits. There are now color consultants in every city, but if you study *Shades of Beauty* and use the color charts included, you will be able to analyze yourself.

Whatever your particular needs, start looking for an answer. Write down a list of your goals and find people who can help you. Don't be afraid to ask questions. No one will think you are stupid. Many of us are full of answers waiting for some questions to come our way!

Although physical improvement is not the only solution for depression, it is a good place to start.

Question 4: What steps do you need to take to lift your self-image?

_____

_____

5. *Help someone else.* Much of our drift into depression comes from preoccupation with self. We are so deeply involved with our own problems that we can't see other people in need; yet when we do help someone else, we get a lift. I have a friend, Betty Lou, who has every reason in the world to be depressed. Her husband has been seriously ill with emphysema for several years. He is connected to an oxygen tank and

occasionally has to be rushed to the hospital for emergency treatment. Besides caring for her husband, she has an 85-year-old mother living with her who is confined to a wheelchair. Betty Lou has also assumed the responsibility to encourage her widowed sister, who lost her only son in a Rocky Mountain avalanche. With all these sad situations, Betty Lou still finds time to help other people. One day when she brought me a big bag of oranges she had picked, I asked her how she had time or strength to visit me.

"When my problems look hopeless, I find someone else to help," she said. "I take my eyes off myself and I cheer up."

My friend Kitty had an ileostomy. This drastic surgery was enough to depress anyone, but Kitty refused to sit around in self-pity. As soon as she could, she set out to help others, and now volunteers many hours a week to counsel those who are distraught over impending surgery.

Another friend, Ruth, has some serious effects from cobalt treatments on her neck, yet she spends at least one full day a week in the hospital encouraging individuals whose loved ones are in surgery. Both Kitty and Ruth have reason to be depressed, but are too busy helping others to notice.

Question 5: How much time do you spend each week in helping others? Remember: NO PURPOSE = NO ACCOMPLISHMENT = DEPRESSION.

6. *Review your financial position.* There are many depressed women who live in lavish homes, charge their clothes at expensive stores, and drive to the country club in a Cadillac. They have made the great American climb, yet are nervous. They may worry over their husband's business, the second mortgage, or a bank loan. It's surprising how easy it is to be depressed

while elegantly gowned at the charity ball if your phone may be disconnected tomorrow. It can be uncomfortable sitting in your 600-dollar damask wing chair if the decorator is threatening to pick it up in the morning. It can be upsetting to answer your French Provincial phone if you know it's another collection agency looking for money.

It's not easy to take a step backward, but sometimes circumstances force us to reevaluate our lifestyle. I know: I did it.

Fred and I built up our business and planned our dream house in the foothills of San Bernardino. We designed and decorated it until we produced a showplace that charity groups used for home tours. We entertained lavishly and frequently and took in strays who needed a home.

Then our circumstances changed. Our food service business ran into problems. Wholesale food prices went up sharply and we were locked into contract feeding without a way to raise our prices. We lost money on every plate we served. If we asked for increases, the contracts would be put out for open bid. If we hung on, we might be able to ride it out. We tried the latter and watched money disappear into thin air. At the same time a new restaurant we had designed and built was also losing money. After 23 years in the business we had to close up and admit defeat.

At 46 Fred had to start again and I had to find a way to supplement his income. It's easy to be depressed while pacing the hall of a six-bedroom home with a sensational view knowing all the time you can't afford to live under its roof. It's easy to stay depressed if we don't reevaluate our lifestyle and take curative action.

We wrote down our monthly expenses and anticipated income. If we both worked ourselves to death, we could make it. We could maintain a semblance of our social standards by pouring everything into our day-to-day existence, or we could make a change. We prayed about our problem, but it was still hard to think about our well-chosen furniture being sold and someone else living in our custom-tailored home.

It was hard, but we decided to list our home and prayed that the house would sell quickly if it was right for us to move. It sold in a week.

Instead of being depressed and focusing on the negatives, a peace came in our hearts. We had prayed; our prayers had been answered; we moved.

From our 3600 square feet, five of us moved to a 1350-square-foot condominium. From a family room that could seat 90 people for Bible studies and a large living room, dining room, and foyer, we went to one all-purpose family, living, and dining room.

For those of you who are a little shaky over your finances, I offer you a solution. Analyze your income and expenses. Look at the figures. Is there an item that is out of proportion? Are you charging yourself into a hole? Are you living beyond your present means?

No wonder you are nervous and discouraged. What are your alternatives? Should you make a move as we did?

Are you afraid your friends will look down on you if you change your lifestyle? Is pride getting in the way of good sense?

I had to deal with all these problems, and I know we made the right choice. I'd rather be cheerful in a condominium than miserable in a mansion. How about you?

Question 6: Are financial problems pressuring you?

7

When You Need
Outside Help

According to the severity of your depression, you may have already found help or you may need additional counsel. If you are so distraught that getting organized and raising your self-image are beyond you, perhaps you should seek outside help.

What kind of assistance is available?

1. *Your family doctor or pastor.* If possible, start with someone who has some personal knowledge of you. Tell him clearly that you are depressed. Don't hide your symptoms or your suicidal tendencies. After you have listed your feelings, listen for his advice. He may arrange for some counseling sessions, refer you to someone better suited to handle your problem, or administer some type of drug.

2. *Mood-elevating drugs.* Antidepressant drugs are now the most popular choice of doctors and psychiatrists for treating serious depressions. Lithium carbonate was invented in 1950 and has proven to be effective in at least 10 to 20 percent of the cases used. Some figures boost it as high as 80 percent, although no exact

statistics are available. Other drugs, such as Tofranil, Elavil, Marplan, and Nardil, are often used, but obviously the administration of such medicines must be carefully monitored by a competent physician. Use of these drugs may give side effects such as dizziness, headaches, drowsiness, excessive perspiration, and high blood pressure. None of these medications should be prescribed without a thorough examination and evaluation.

Dr. Nathan Kline, who wrote *From Sad to Glad* and who has worked with these drugs since the '50's at Rockland State Hospital in New York, cautions against the automatic administration of drugs without enough groundwork. He first spends time with each patient: "When a patient describes his symptoms, I am listening not just to his words but also to his tone, and I am observing the nuances of his posture, dress and general manner. Drug treatment of the depression consists of much more than prescribing pills. One must treat the whole patient while dealing with many human facets of the disease."

One great caution for those who use drugs to lift their spirits: Such drug treatment is for the symptoms, not the cause. While depression may ease with drug use, the underlying problem may not change and may even lead to deeper depression when the effect of the drugs wears off.

3. *The National Institute of Mental Health.* The NIMH has material on depression available and will send a directory of federally funded mental health centers upon request. The centers have trained workers and round-the-clock emergency services to help those in need. For further information write: NIMH, 5600 Fishers Lane, Rockville, Maryland 20857.

4. *Psychotherapy.* Many psychiatrists feel the best

way to bring about healing is to delve deeply into the patient's past and his subconscious to discover the cause of the patient's depression. Psychotherapy has been effective in many cases, but it is hardly a quick solution and can be expensive. One of the dangers of consulting a psychiatrist who is not a Christian is that he may consider our beliefs to be narrow and straitlaced and go on a personal crusade to loosen us up.

5. *Group therapy.* Many people who share their problems in a group situation receive an instant "pick-up" when they discover that other people are also suffering from depression. Some people, however, are embarrassed to share their deep feelings and become more depressed. Others become so dependent on the group that they withdraw from normal social relationships.

6. *Alcoholics Anonymous.* This is one of the best-known support groups. Its aim is to have people who have been addicted and recovered minister to those with similar needs by showing them, "I've been there. I know what you're going through. I've made it and so can you." There is now a variety of these groups: Emotions Anonymous, Overeaters Anonymous, Cocaine Anonymous. Whenever a problem of magnitude arises, support groups are formed. One of our CLASS staff, Jan Frank, has started several support groups for incest victims and now speaks instructing others on how to set up such groups for their needs. When people of similar problems get together and share what worked for them, there is a sense of close fellowship and mutual support. Georgia Venard, also of CLASS staff, has her Tuesday night group for Christians who have been on drugs.

7. *Electroconvulsive therapy (ECT).* Shock treatment, used much more frequently 15 years ago than

today, can give instant and dramatic improvement to those who are deeply depressed or suicidal. I had one friend who tried to kill herself and was given one ECT that brought her back to reality. After several treatments she was released from the hospital and has never had a relapse. Dr. Gerald Klerman of Harvard says, "We still need convulsive therapy, particularly for the severely afflicted, or for those whom drugs have already failed, or for the intensely suicidal patient who should not wait days or weeks for drugs to work. Fortunately, there is a small number of such patients."

It is important to realize that the long-range effect of ECT on the brain is still unknown. Some patients suffer from troublesome side effects such as upset stomach, memory loss, and mental confusion. Obviously, this drastic measure should be used judiciously and only in extreme cases.

8. *Stress analysis.* In recent years many tests have been devised to help doctors chart the cause or severity of depression. One is a stress analysis, mentioned earlier, and another is the Beck Depression Inventory, in which a person suspected of depression is asked to rate himself on 21 symptom categories. From the answers given to these analyses, a doctor should have some important clues as to why the person is depressed. You should know, however, that the intuition and ability of the doctor plays a major role in the effectiveness of these tools.

A Newport, Rhode Island, psychiatrist, Dr. Colette Cunningham, has said, "Stress may have caused the breast cancer in Betty Ford and Happy Rockefeller and a stroke suffered by Pat Nixon."

Dr. Cunningham told a Federal Women's week luncheon, "Stress can trigger diabetes, cancer and hypertension as well as alcoholism and drug addiction."

She pointed out, "Mrs. Ford and Mrs. Rockefeller both developed breast cancer shortly after arduous campaigning for their husbands. Mrs. Nixon had a stroke after Watergate."

Unrecognized and untreated stress can be the cause of both depression and physical ailments.

9. *Electronic tests.* Experts at the Massachusetts General Hospital and Harvard University have found a way to measure minute facial muscles electronically. By the use of electrodes laid on the patient's face, doctors can now tell who is really depressed. While this new machine is a definite improvement in the diagnosis of depression, it does not measure the cause or provide a solution.

Another machine, developed at the University of Wisconsin Medical School, is a computer designed to predict suicides. Programmed by psychiatrist John Greist and professor David Gustafson, the computer correctly identified three patients who attempted suicide within 48 hours after their test. *Time* magazine (July 24, 1978) reported:

> One patient was about to be released when the computer determined that he had a gun, bullets and a precise suicide plan. In long-range predictions, covering nine months after the interviews, the computer identified 90 percent of the actual suicide attempters, compared with 30 percent for the therapists."

10. *Biofeedback.* In recent years the new experience of biofeedback has been used to train individuals to control their own stress and some types of depression. An article on stress in *Mademoiselle*, March 1978, explains the technique this way:

Biofeedback training is simply an electronic extension of the way we normally learn. It involves getting cues from our senses that become self-correcting.

When electrodes are attached to points on the body, the effect of thoughts and feelings can be easily displayed on a TV-type screen as a series of blips, lines or beeps. The patient, while watching the monitor, is asked to try and relax, slow down his heart rate or reduce his blood pressure. The patient gets a continuous and instant "check" on what his body is doing when he behaves in certain ways.

Biofeedback is obviously a specialized science still in its infancy. I talked with one girl who had been treated by this method. She told me she had learned to relax so well that after one visit she sat down on a bench to wait for a bus, fell asleep immediately, and slept for six hours.

There are many avenues which we can pursue to gain greater understanding of the problems we face. The outside help we find is a tool in God's hands to encourage us or give us deeper insight. However, the ultimate answer always rests in His Word and in the transforming love of God.

8

Nobody Knows the Troubles I've Seen

While positive thinking, purposeful action, and the counsel of good doctors can help the depressed person, I have witnessed the greatest changes in the "total person" through spiritual help. During the years I've spent speaking and counseling, I have become convinced that the Bible is the greatest psychology manual ever written. The reason more of us don't turn to the Bible in times of trouble is because we don't know where to look for the answers. I have searched out spiritual solutions to depression and have applied them to myself and others with successful results.

Dr. Walter Johnson of Hanover, Massachusetts, wrote me a letter after listening to my tape *Defeating Depression*. From his years of experience in caring for the sick and depressed he wrote:

> Although I am convinced, and indeed scientific evidence is very strong in this area, that in many cases biological factors are a predominant cause of depression, I am very insistent that spiritual counseling is of the utmost

importance in treating depressed individuals,
in conjunction when necessary with antidepressant medications, etc. I could give you
numerous examples of instances in which this
combined approach has been most helpful.

For those of you who want more than a human
purpose for the day or a pill for a pickup, let me present
a permanent plan for peace of mind.

1. *Believe the Bible.* Before we can use the Bible as
our textbook, we have to believe it is God's Word.

First Corinthians 2:14 tells us the Bible is foolishness
to those who do not believe. We must believe in *God*,
the Father who created us; in *Jesus Christ*, the Son of
God who died for our sins; and in the *Holy Spirit*, the
available power who can change our patterns of life.
When we do *believe*, we can with assurance follow
God's plan for overcoming depression.

Many people have a vague belief in some divine
authority, but few have a personal spiritual relationship
that really works. I spent my childhood in Sunday
school and church activities. I led the youth group and
went to religious conferences. As an adult I regularly
attended church and considered myself a Christian,
mainly because I wasn't anything else; yet when I was
faced with the tragedy of two brain-damaged sons,
being able to recite the books of the Bible didn't provide
much consolation. I prayed for healing for my sons,
but knew it was hopeless. Soon whatever faith I had
disappeared and I decided there couldn't be a God if
a good person like me was in such a situation.

I quit believing in anything, and the last thing I
wanted was for anyone to tell me I needed religion. I
didn't need religion; I needed a relationship with Jesus
Christ as a Person, but I didn't know how to find Him.

I didn't know where to turn for help, so I sat home hopeless and depressed. Some of you may really want the power of a spiritual experience, but have no idea how to find it. You've been a churchgoer, but sitting in a pew pretending to be happy hasn't helped.

When I got to the point where I knew there was absolutely nothing I could do to resurrect my dead son or remake my retarded one, I gave up. Little did I know that giving up on myself was the beginning of a cure for my depression.

2. *Give yourself away.* Since the key problem in depression is an absorption with self, we have to get our eyes off ourselves. Humanly speaking, this is close to impossible, for by the time we realize we are depressed the sky has fallen in around us and we can't see anything but ourselves and our problem. How can we look for the flowers when we're choked up with weeds? How could I go to a supermarket and smile at little boys in their mothers' carts when I knew my Frederick Jerome Littauer III was dead and my Laurence Chapman Littauer was dying? I couldn't go anywhere without shocking reminders of my misery. Until one day. . .

My sister-in-law Ruthie, who was concerned for my depressed state, took me to a Christian Women's Club. I didn't want to go and I didn't intend to listen to the speaker; yet, when a tall, distinguished gentleman stood up, I listened. He told a story of a woman like me who was unhappy. She was a good person who even went to church, but she didn't know how to receive spiritual power in her life. I didn't either.

The speaker quoted Romans 12:1,2: "Present your bodies a living sacrifice, holy, acceptable unto God, which is your reasonable service. And be not conformed to this world, but be transformed by the renewing of your mind, that ye may prove what is that good and acceptable and perfect will of God for you." I had heard this before, but, as with all my Bible knowledge, it didn't mean anything to me personally. He said there might be ladies in the audience who needed help, and I nodded my head.

Then these thoughts came through to me. I should *present my body*. I should *give myself away*. To whom? To God through Jesus Christ. I had already given up on myself, so now I had to give myself away to the Lord Jesus. "Why not?" I thought. "I'm a failure anyway. Why keep me around?"

I didn't think I was giving away much of a prize, nor did I think the Lord was going to be too excited to add one more gloomy girl to His group. I decided to donate myself anyway.

Be not conformed to the world. I had spent my life working on worldly standards. I had planned a career in teaching followed by a perfect marriage and perfect children. I wanted to live up to the best standards the world had to offer. I had such good motives, yet I had produced two brain-damaged sons and the world had no answers. Conforming to the world had not helped me, so what had I to lose?

Be transformed. The verse told me that when I gave myself to the Lord and quit worrying about the world, God would transform me. How I needed a change, a new life! How I needed to get beyond my personal gloom to a higher plane! How I needed more than the happy pills the doctors had offered! God promised to renew my mind; I was ready to take Him up on it.

Know God's will. Then you will know (how I needed to be *sure* of something!) what is that good, acceptable, and perfect will of God for you. I didn't think God even knew me. I surely had never known Him in a personal way, but I was willing to become acquainted with any power that could transform me from hopelessness to health, that could give me a new mind and a new direction.

I prayed right there in that restaurant. Religion needs the ritual of a church, but a spiritual relationship can start in a restaurant. I asked Jesus Christ to come into my life and give me a new mind. I also asked that He show me clearly what God's plan for my discouraged life should be.

Once I made this commitment to the Lord I felt better. For the first time I knew I was a Christian, not because I wasn't something else but because I had given myself to Christ.

How many of you reading this book would like to get rid of yourselves? How many have thought of running away? Leaving town? Ending it all? How many have tried grand plans and marvelous medications and are ready to chuck it all?

I know where you are; I've been there. I might be there yet, but I gave myself away. I took my eyes off myself and put them on the Lord. I called upon the name of Jesus and was saved from a sad life with myself.

Why not *believe* in God's Word today and *give* yourself to Jesus?

3. *Realize that you are not alone.* Before I began to *believe* for real and before I *gave* myself away, I thought I was the only person with deep problems. Other people had little problems, but I was the one with the big problems. I was especially the only one in the world who had produced two brain-damaged sons. Who could top that? Can you? Perhaps you feel your situation is worse. Perhaps you think no one else but you is so depressed. Nobody know the troubles I've seen—nobody knows but Jesus.

As I began to study the Bible for help I found a verse that spoke to me. First Corinthians 10:13 says, "There hath no temptation [problem, trial, depression] taken you but such as is common to man; but God is faithful, who will not allow you to be tested above that you are able, but will with the trial also make a way of escape, that you may be able to bear it."

What comfort I received from that verse! The first thing it told me is that I am not the only one to have such a problem. I really thought I was. Since I have been sharing my life story in public, I have had many women tell me tragic tales of their retarded children and ruined lives. I was not alone with this problem, nor are you. Whatever has you down today is not a peculiar problem. Others have had this trial before, others are going through it today, and still others will have it fall upon them tomorrow.

Somehow that knowledge helped me, and I hope it will help you too. We are not the first, last, or only ones to go through difficult times. Many depressed ladies tell me, "My case is different from anyone else's." It may be a different cast on a different stage in different costumes, but the plot is the same. Something has gone wrong in our lives and we can't stand it any longer.

The verse jumps in with the assurance, "but God is faithful." We may be troubled, vacillating, and even thinking of running away, but God is faithful. He will not allow this problem to go beyond what we are able to handle. Once we give ourselves to the Lord He watches over us; He doesn't let things go too far.

If I had written the Bible I would have put things differently: I would have given each committed believer an easy life. But God did not see it my way; He planned life on earth to be a testing ground for our future. As a parent toward a child he loves, God chastens us for our own good. He allows us to go through trials to perfect our character.

James asks such an appropriate question: "Is your life full of difficulties and temptations? Then be happy, for when the way is rough, your patience has a chance to grow. So let it grow, and don't try to squirm out of your problems. For when your patience is finally in full bloom, then you will be ready for anything, strong in character, full and complete" (James 1:2-4 TLB).

We don't need to squirm out of our difficulties, but face them, knowing that God is faithful and that He will not allow us to be tested too far. He does not promise us a rose garden, but He does say that with the trial He will provide us a way of escape. When I first read that word "escape" I was encouraged. God was going to help me run away from my problems, skirt around them, or tunnel under them; but then I looked at the last clause: ". . . that you may be able to bear it." To bear anything you have to stay with it. These thoughts seemed contradictory, so I hunted up the word "escape" in its original use and found that it means to be lifted above the problem enough to get a more detached perspective. This escape is what God has for us: He will pick us up from the depth of our depression and give us an objective view of our situation so that we will be able to bear it, not run away from it.

I wish God promised each believer a perfect life, but He didn't. He did, however, comfort us by saying we aren't the only one with this problem, He is always faithful, He won't let the suffering go too far, and He will lift us above the eye of the storm "that we will be able to bear it."

When I began to realize I wasn't alone in my problems, and that other people besides me had deep troubles, my pain began to ease. When I went further and saw I wasn't alone because God was with me to lift my spirits, I was encouraged. I had sat too long alone. I had resisted friends and activities to sink silently into my own special sadness. Now I could know that God in His infinite wisdom had a plan for me. And He does for you too.

Once we *believe* in the words of the Bible and in God the Father, the Son, and the Holy Spirit, and once we *give* ourselves to the Lord Jesus for His control, He will begin to work out His plan for our lives *if* we are willing.

4. *Desire a change.* Before God can do much with us, we have to be willing. I have learned in counseling women with problems that the greatest solutions in the world are worth nothing if the individual isn't willing to take a first step. I had to take a giant step myself.

As I began to work on my new life, I realized that being a Christian is not just going to church and being a nice person. It is a total commitment of a life to the Lord and a willingness to let Him make you into what He wants you to be. Many people fear that in giving their lives to God He will present them with a big list of don'ts and their fun will be over. I found that He doesn't give don'ts but *changes desires.*

As I began to study God's Word, it spoke to me in a personal way and I soon found that I wanted to please my husband. I realized that in all my years of marriage I had been trying to please *me*. I had accepted my husband's directions, but resented them, and did only enough to barely get along with him. No wonder we drifted apart in time of tragedy!

One day my daughter Lauren said, "I hope I never have to grow up and get married and be miserable like you." I was stunned that she would say such a thing, as I had always played the role of the perfect wife. "What do you mean?" I asked.

She replied, "Well, you're always complaining." I knew I wasn't and told her so. "You may not think you're complaining," she said, "but all the time you're doing the dishes, you're saying to yourself how you hate dishes, how Daddy's always late, and how you were made for better things than this."

I couldn't believe I had ever said such things, but I soon became aware that I muttered around the house with everything I did. While the pressures of our sons had relaxed, I was still depressed. I tried to be the life of the party outside of the home, but inside my children saw me as a bitter, angry, complaining woman. I began to pray that God would change my attitudes and show me my faults. When I was willing, He was able.

As I began to apply the Bible truths I was learning, I became more and more aware of my areas of need. I was definitely a *believer*. The Bible was no longer foolishness, and I was confident that God could turn my negative attitudes into positive ones. But how?

I had grown comfortable in my depression. I quit my social and civic activities, withdrew from many of my friends, and resigned myself to never having another son. I made sure of this by having a hysterectomy. When I accepted the fact that the good life had passed me by, it was easier to sit around in my understandable depression than to do anything about it.

Yet my life could be better. I had given myself to the Lord, and knew I was no longer alone, but was I willing to take a big step of faith? Did I really want a change? I decided I did.

My husband had been deeply wounded by his failure to produce normal sons and had escaped into his work. As long as he was fully occupied he didn't have to think about his problems. Only when he came home to the empty crib was he overwhelmed with grief.

I saw very little of Fred in these troubled times. I was truly alone. When I had an occasional dinner with him, I began to ask his views on adoption. He didn't care to have someone else's baby, but he agreed to apply if it would make me happy. I desired a change and my request was answered: a bright and healthy three-month-old boy—a new Freddie.

While a new baby does not guarantee happiness, Freddie represented my first tangible step toward recovery.

As I took my eyes off myself and got on with life, my husband noticed a difference in me. He became willing to take a new step. We started going to a church where the pastor taught from the Bible, and soon Fred committed his life to the Lord. When we were willing to change, God was able to work in our hearts. *When we are willing, He is able!*

Where do you stand today? Are you ready to throw away your depression, your anger, your bitterness, your selfishness, your old bathrobe that has been with you so long? Or are you going to hang tightly onto your problems in hopes that the world will change?

Governor George Wallace, confined to a wheelchair after an assassin's attempt on his life, was in a state of deep depression. His hopes for the presidency were dashed and he felt there was nothing to live for. One day the editor of the *Montgomery Advertiser* printed a request for Wallace to retire from being governor, and this shocked him into a new desire for a change. A friend said, "A large part of his trouble was mental. Once he decided to crawl out of the depression, he did it."

Beverly came to me one day with a problem. She was

depressed because she and her husband had each been married three times and their current relationship was in deep trouble. One of the symptoms was that Bob got angry every time he reached in his drawers and had no socks. Each morning he would storm downstairs, stamp through the house to the dryer, and pull out a pair. Since she washed the black socks and white T-shirts together, the shirts were gray and the socks had white balls of fuzz all over them. She couldn't be bothered with laundry, but Bob was a neat, meticulous dresser and would blow up every time he saw the condition of his socks.

One doesn't have to be brilliant to come up with a solution to this problem. I gave Beverly a simple answer. However, when I asked if she was willing to wash his socks and T-shirts in separate tubs and then take them all to his drawers, she said, "No."

I asked her if she was willing to be willing and she said, "No."

I then tried, "Are you willing to be willing to be willing?"

She smiled and said, "All right, I'll go for three willings."

I gave her a verse from Philippians 2:13: "God is *always* at work in you *to make you willing* and able to obey his own purpose" (TEV).

"Is it God's purpose that you hold this third marriage together?" I asked. She agreed that it was. "Then He will make you willing," I said. I suggested that she memorize the verse and apply it to her life.

When she returned the following week, she said, "I'm down to two willings." The third week she was *really* willing! She had washed the socks separately, had folded them in pairs, and had taken them as far as the stairs. Her husband, thrilled that she had gotten them that far, agreed to carry them to his dresser drawers. The next week he came for counsel and *both were willing* to resolve their remaining differences.

What about you? Are you willing? Do you really desire a change in whatever your problem might be? Why not memorize Philippians 2:13 and believe that God is always—not just occasionally when He feels like it, but always—at work in YOU! He's in there with you, helping you and making you willing. He wants you to be willing, to desire the very best. He wants you to be able to obey His good purpose. He *will* make you *able* to do His will. Is it God's will that you be depressed or joyful? Angry or pleasant? Bitter or loving? Will you allow Him to make you willing?

5. *Deal with your guilt.* Many psychiatrists feel that a guilty conscience is sitting at the bottom of each depression. Because we feel guilty we can never be completely free. When the little black cloud of guilt rides with us, we can't relax in the sunlight. Although it's generally agreed that guilt is a serious problem, no simple cure has been invented. Happy pills may brighten us up for the moment, but when we miss a dose the guilt comes back.

Is there a spiritual way to handle guilt? Yes, there is; I've used it.

First, we must divide our guilt in two categories: justified and unnecessary. As you read this right now ask God to bring to your mind the things you feel guilty about and write them down. Keep writing until you can't think of anything more. Now go back over the list. After each item ask yourself, "Do I feel guilty about this because I really am guilty? Are my emotions justified? Have I really done something wrong?" Where the answer is "yes," put a checkmark.

Now let's deal with your justified guilt. Do you

have some items like this in your column?

I feel guilty because:

I don't write my mother.
I won't visit my in-laws.
I don't speak to Joe in the office.
I'm having an affair with the choir director.

Your guilts are doubtless more creative, but let's look at these.

I don't write my mother. This was a justified guilt in my life. When my mother was 80 she lived alone in Massachusetts. I was in California, one brother was in Dallas, and the other was in Japan. When I think of how hard she worked to get us through school I realize she sacrificed a great deal of her life for us. Was it asking too much that we write?

When I analyze this guilt, I have to confess I was guilty. As soon as we find a justified guilt, we must act to remove it. What did I do? I started writing my mother at least once a week and sending her postcards wherever I went.

I won't go visit my in-laws. One day I was counseling Carolyn on her depression. At one point she said, "I feel a little guilty about my in-laws. I just won't go visit them. They do nothing but complain. Besides, they are crude and offensive." Her guilt was justified, but since she had always put the blame on them for their unattractive behavior, she had never faced the fact that she might be wrong. Yet the guilt hung on.

The Bible tells us that when we marry we are to leave our father and mother and cleave to our partner (Genesis 2:24). We are not to let our parents or in-laws run our lives, yet we are to treat them with respect.

We are to keep in touch and visit them when possible regardless of their attitude or response to us. We don't go to visit because they are charming (which hopefully they are) but because we are commanded to honor our father and our mother (Deuteronomy 5:16). The Bible doesn't say, "Be nice if they deserve it."

God only holds us accountable for our own actions, not other people's reactions. Once I understood this truth, my Christian life took a giant step forward. As long as I am doing what's right, I don't have to worry whether the response is enthusiastic.

Fred's grandfather started each of our visits with, "How long are you going to stay?" If our answer was two hours or two weeks, his grumbled response was always the same: "Is that all?"

That opening could discourage one from visiting, but his attitude was not our problem. We were not there to receive credit or praise. Once we got this perspective into our minds, we enjoyed our time more. We didn't get offended and he seemed more relaxed. When we accepted him exactly as he was, he liked us better.

Do you have in-law problems? Sit down with your mate and work out a plan. How often will you visit each family? What holidays will you have with them? When will you have them over for dinner?

Make an equitable arrangement and then stay with it no matter what their reaction. They may feign heart attacks and threaten to die, but if you are fair, don't be afraid to be firm. I know one couple who for five years kept postponing their wedding because each time they announced the date, the bride's mother would end up in the hospital with stomach ulcers. Finally they announced they were getting married even if the mother was in the hospital. Bravely they went on with their plans, and the mother showed up at the wedding in good health.

If you feel guilty about your treatment of your in-laws, analyze your guilt. If it is justified, make it right by them. Honor your father and mother regardless of their reactions or personalities, and God will bless your obedience.

I don't speak to Joe in the office. And with good reason. Joe pulled a nasty deal on me and I haven't spoken to him since. What a perfect way to keep a black cloud hovering over the office! You and Joe avoid each other and the secretaries take sides. This exact problem took place at Norton Air Force Base where I taught a Bible study for many years.

One day I was speaking on guilt and forgiveness and referred to Matthew 5:23,24: "If you are about to offer your gift to God at the altar and there you remember that your brother has something against you, leave your gift there in front of the altar, go at once to make peace with your brother, and then come back and offer your gift to God" (TEV). I explained that it was possible for us to be sitting in a Bible study giving our attention to God and yet have a grudge against someone or know someone is upset with us. According to this verse, God doesn't want our gift until we've straightened out our human relationship.

As soon as the class was over Rod whipped out the door. By the time I had said goodbye to the others he was back. "I did just what you said. I've been mad at Joe for months, and so I went right down to our office and told him I was sorry I hadn't spoken to him. He was amazed and said he was sorry about what he'd done. I feel better already."

Perhaps you are depressed by some guilt you know

you could do something about. Look over your list and get moving.

I'm having an affair with the choir director. I chose this line because I've had too many sweet church ladies confess that they are fooling around with a saintly leader of the flock and then wonder why they feel guilty. God equipped us with a conscience to keep us out of trouble. When we sense we're heading for dangerous waters our conscience begins to twinge. However, if we rationalize the temptation long enough, we can justify it: "If you had a husband like mine you'd run around too." Once we enter blithely into a situation we know is wrong, guilt also moves in, and depression always follows.

I've come up with a practical rule to teach my children about temptation: "If in doubt, don't!"

One depressed lady called me in my motel room in San Francisco and said she needed to talk with me. I met her for breakfast, and as I ate my scrambled eggs she told me a tale of intrigue. It all started at choir rehearsal. She had fallen in love with the director. Although both were married, she was intrigued with his looks. "It never hurts to look," she said. She had volunteered to pass out songbooks and he thanked her by patting her on the shoulder. She interpreted this as a seductive act and sat next to him when the choir went out for coffee. She took a passionate interest in singing and asked for extra help. One night when they were alone in the choir loft a key clicked in the front door and both ducked down behind the organ.

"Crouched with him in a tight corner was the most exciting moment of my life," she said. "That's when it all started."

This was not, of course, when it all started, but it surely picked up from there.

Here was a good woman who meant well and knew better, but who had gotten herself involved in a scandalous situation and felt guilty. This was justifiable guilt that had to be dealt with.

The first step was to stop singing—at least in that choir—and to change churches. She had to stop seeing the choir director at any time or place and set her heart on her husband.

If you are playing with matches you may start a fire, and when the fireman catches you with the evidence in your hands, you'll feel guilty.

When in doubt, don't!

Look over your list once more. How many of your guilts are justifiable? Are you willing to do something about them?

Betty Wright from Riverside wrote me her suggestion:

> If you have a deep sense of guilt, list all those people you feel you have wronged, no matter how far back in your life or how trivial it may seem. If you feel guilty about it, it's important to be free of the guilt. Pray over the list. Ask God to remind you of any you may have left out. Ask God to forgive you for each wrong. Begin to seek the forgiveness of each wronged individual. If it's a loved one, relative, or family, a phone call is great. Otherwise, tell the Lord you want to ask these people's forgiveness, and believe me, He will bring you in contact with them. Don't phone or write those whom it might embarrass or trouble. Remember, you are trying to free yourself from guilt, not add more.

What about your leftover guilts? These are probably

unnecessary guilts put there by other people who appear to mean well but enjoy seeing you wilt and crawl. One friend of mine is a perfect example of a person weighted down with unnecessary guilt. Bobbie was involved in a tragic accident a few years ago. Her recovery has been difficult and has been impeded by the constant advice of her church friends. "If you were really spiritual, you would force yourself to go to our Bible studies, where we could help you." "If you cared about your daughter, you would drive her to choir practice." "If you were a good wife, you would answer the phone for your husband's business and save him the money he pays for that secretary. In fact, after seeing her figure I think you're stupid to even have her around."

Such charitable suggestions heaped dear Bobbie with unnecessary guilt. At a time when she needed emotional encouragement, her friends were giving her a guilty conscience.

There is nothing we can do about changing our friends' behavior, but we can deal with unnecessary guilt in a spiritual way. When someone tries to make you feel guilty, thank him for the suggestion and tell him you will certainly give it serious consideration. If it has merit, think about it; if it does not, ask the Lord to quickly remove even the memory of the statement from you.

When Bobbie told me of the friends and relatives who had told her she should be helping in the business, I asked, "Does your husband want you to work for him?"

She said, "When I told him what they said he laughed. He told me he wouldn't let me go to work even if I felt able."

Bobbie checked out her friends' suggestion, received

her husband's answer, and even found the "shapely secretary" to be a customer whom a friend had misjudged. In the process she removed the unnecessary guilt and anxiety that was detrimental to her recovery.

How much of your guilt is unnecessary? Are people expecting more of you than you can handle? Are people pressuring you into positions you have no time for? Are people judging you according to their own narrow standards?

You can't please everyone. You can only do the best you know how to under the circumstances and not worry about what people think. Ask the Lord right now to remove all the guilt that has been put upon you by other people.

God does not want us laden with unnecessary guilt, and He pledges to relieve us when we ask. Hebrews 10:22,23 states: "Let us come near to God with a sincere heart and a sure faith, with hearts that have been purified from a guilty conscience and with bodies washed with clean water. Let us hold on firmly to the hope we profess, because we can trust God to keep his promise" (TEV).

After I committed my life to the Lord and desired relief from my depression, I still held onto unnecessary guilt. I didn't know what to label it and had no one to help me uncover my problem. Relatives told me that Freddie had probably been dropped by some babysitter while I was out seeking pleasure. Christians solemnly stated, "God is punishing you for your sins." (This statement is guaranteed to drop a person several steps on the depression scale.) Friends couldn't imagine how we could put our children away and forget them. Others said that if I were really a good mother I would devote my life to Larry's care. When you are already in a state of hopelessness, none of these comments do much to encourage you. Gratefully, the Lord showed me how to deal with my guilt: "Is there any validity to the statement? Are you doing the best you can about your problems? Then give the guilt to Me and stop worrying about the people."

I looked over my list. Freddie had not been dropped on his head; he and Larry both had some genetic brain damage. It had nothing to do with my being a neglectful mother and there was no point in my bearing that heavy burden.

God does not inflict damages upon us to give us a bad time. He does use our problems to develop our character, and through the loss of my sons I realized my need for a spiritual relationship. I had failed to salvage two sons in my own power and I gave myself to the Lord. Whatever sin I might be guilty of He had forgiven.

How could we put our children away? How could we afford not to? Each child was beyond repair or hope, each was too sick to know his own mother, and each needed 24-hour nursing care. Each had constant convulsions and screamed night and day.

Should we have kept them home and ruined the lives of our two normal girls? Should we have listened to their continual crying and settled into a life of gloom and despair?

Fred and I discussed our decision and felt we made the right choice. Why now, years later, should I be made to feel guilty by people who had never been in my shoes?

Without even knowing what I was doing, I gave these unnecessary guilts to the Lord and He took them away. Furthermore, He has used me to help other people and never once has He condemned me. He kept a promise I didn't even know He had made.

Before you go any further, make sure you have looked over those patchwork guilts that are covering up your joy. Then ask the Lord to fold them up and put them away in a distant closet. Believe Him when He says they are gone. Don't go hunting for them again. They're the Lord's property. And we have the promise in Hebrews 9:14 that He will make our consciences clean. Don't spend another moment with unnecessary guilt when there are joyful companions available.

6. *Confess your depression.* The word "confess" means "to acknowledge or admit a fault or a problem." The Bible calls these faults or problems *sins* and tells us that God already knows them. All we have to do is agree with Him. He doesn't tell us that because we have faults, depressions, or sins we are rotten people with hopeless lives. Rather, when we're willing to admit we have a problem, He'll forgive us and wipe out the burden. No human can do this for us! I can confess to a friend and she might sympathize, but only the Lord Jesus can take away the pain.

When my problems overwhelmed me, friends tried to cheer me up, but since no one could restore my boys, nothing they did restored my joy. One day I read 1 John 1:9,10 and saw that there was a conditional hope for me: "If we confess our sins to God, he will keep his promise and do what is right: he will forgive us our sins and purify us from all our wrongdoing. If we say that we have not sinned, we make a liar out of God, and his word is not in us" (TEV).

As I thought about these words I realized I had carried my depression too far. I hadn't thought I had sinned because the circumstances were beyond my control, but now I realized I was wrong in letting bad circumstances turn me into a mournful mother and a weeping wife. I came to understand that I wasn't responsible for my situation but was responsible for my reaction to it.

I was uncomfortable with the word "sin." I thought it applied only to bank robbers and flagrant fornicators, neither of which I was. However, I found that the Scriptural definition of sin is *everything not in conformity to God's will in purpose, thought, and action.* I could see that it wasn't God's will for me to be constantly grieving over my lost sons, to hurt my two girls with my crying, or to be so gloomy that my husband didn't want to come home. I accepted verse 10, which said that if I refused to believe I had sinned I was calling God a liar. Once I was willing to accept God at His Word, He was able to deal with me.

I confessed, admitted, and agreed that my depression was a sin, something not in accordance with God's will for my life. I then asked God to forgive me for being gloomy and unproductive for so long and asked Him to clean out all my negative qualities.

When for the first time in my life I acknowledged that my depression was not a natural trait but a sin, God took the burdens away. He didn't change my circumstances; He just made me able to accept them and get on with some new direction. Only then did I experience the release of hopelessness and the enrichment of happiness.

Has your depression and guilt been a burden too long? Is it possible that you're not conforming to God's will and thus thwarting His action? Think about it for a minute. Would you like relief and a fresh start? God has given us this conditional promise: If we confess, He will forgive and cleanse. *If we, then He!*

Confess your depression, agree with God that you are hurting, and know the forgiving, cleansing power of the Lord in your life!

9

Can Black Clouds
Have Silver Linings?

Before we blow away those last black clouds, we must be sure we're connected to the only Source that can save us. A loose belief in a super Being can't change our lives. A lofty position in the local church won't bring peace to a troubled heart. Only the love of the Lord Jesus living in us can lift us above the gloom. In John 1:12 we are assured that when we *believe* in Jesus Christ and receive Him into our lives, He gives us the power to become the real children of God right then. I need that power. How about you?

To be sure of divine direction we must *give* ourselves away to God—present our bodies a living sacrifice: "Here I am, Lord; take me." We must ask God to transform us and give us a new mind. We must ask for His plan for our lives and then accept it.

Next we must *realize* that we are not alone in our dilemmas. Others have faced similar trials in the past and more will in the future, but God is faithful and will give us the power to rise above our problems.

But this happens only when we *desire* a change in

our lives and are willing for the Lord Jesus to start transforming our minds. He is not pushy and won't barge in, even for our own good, until we invite Him.

We must *deal* with our guilts, correct those which are justified, and give up those which interrupt our fellowship with our Lord. Jesus said, "Come to me, all of you who are tired from carrying heavy loads, and I will give you rest" (Matthew 11:28 TEV). We can rejoice in the assurance that when we *confess* our guilts, depressions, problems, and sins to the Lord, He indeed forgives us and cleans us up.

If you have followed these first six steps to spiritual security, the next challenges will provide exciting opportunities for growth.

1. *Forget the past.* Did you know that as committed believers we're able to forget the past? I needed some help in forgetting. Every day I saw the image of my Freddie in his tiny casket. The cry of a child brought the chills of convulsions crashing over me. A ride in the country reminded me of the trip through the hills of Connecticut to place a bandaged baby in the arms of an unknown nurse. The sight of a mother pushing a retarded child in a carriage made me feel sick.

It's true that time heals many wounds, but there is a faster way, Paul tells us in Philippians 3:13, "I . . . forget what is behind me and do my best to reach what is ahead" (TEV). Paul had much to forget. I've never been beaten, shipwrecked, or chained in a jail, but Paul had. He didn't lose two sons, but I did. Whatever our problem, it's worse because it's ours.

When I read that Paul set a goal of forgetting the past, I wondered if I should. Was a good mother to forget her children? Was I to take my eyes off my past? As I prayed over these questions, the Lord comforted me. He showed me that there was absolutely nothing I could do about my son who was dead and almost nothing I could do for Larry. He showed me that brooding over the past kept me from getting on with the future. He showed me that my husband was right in not letting me visit my son. Since I could do nothing to help him, seeing him would only keep me depressed. He showed me that I must forget the past, stamp out the bitterness that had grown up like weeds, and start being a joyful mother to the three children who desperately needed my attention. Once I realized that it was Scripturally right to *forget the past* and get on with the future, my guilt lifted.

When I share this effective principle of forgetting the past, many women share their past with me. Phyllis shared her past that was a past to end all pasts! Her father and mother had both been alcoholics. While the mother watched, her father had beaten and molested her. To escape apprehension the family moved frequently, and Phyllis seldom went to school longer than a few months at a time. Six months before she told me this tale, her mother had stabbed her father to death and then killed herself. Her sister had been picked up on drug charges and her brother had become a homosexual from sleeping all his life with his grandfather. Phyllis married a man who gambled and drank. She left him to live with a friend whose husband later tried to rape her. By the time Phyllis finished the details of this terrible drama and told me she was going to commit suicide, I was ready to join her!

What can you say to a girl with a past like that? There is no human way to forget such a sordid background, but with God all things are possible. Unknowingly, Phyllis made the first positive step by moving away from the town of her traumas. We first established the fact that her most important purpose in life was to forget the past and we then found a new friend to pray with her for this much-needed miracle. She already had a job, so we established some outside goals and plans for raising her self-image. As a Christian believer Phyllis had the power available to lift her above an unforgettable past.

Do you have something on your mind that should be thrown away? Is an unhealthy history keeping you from fulfilling your future? Have you listed the hurts that people have hurled at you? Make it your single purpose to forget what is behind and reach for what's ahead, and God will reward you.

2. *Ask for a silver lining.* Once we throw away the clutter of the past, we have available space to think creatively. It's a principle of physics that two things can't fill one space at the same time. This also applies to our minds. Remember also that happiness comes from good circumstances, but joy comes from Jesus. Why are we depressed? The Lord Himself answers that question in John 16:24: "Hitherto have you asked nothing in my name; ask, and you shall receive, *that your joy may be full."*

Have you directly, clearly, and willingly asked Jesus for *joy*? If you haven't, and don't have joy, Jesus says it's because you haven't asked Him for it.

When I first became a born-again believer, I didn't realize that there was a supernatural joy available to me, but I claimed it when I found this verse. "Lord," I prayed, "You've emptied me of the haunting memories and guilts of the past. Please fill me with Your joy." As I prayed each day for joy, my former love of life returned. I was able to smile again and say for the first time in years, "This is the day which the Lord hath made; I will rejoice and be glad in it" (Psalm 118:24).

We all have problems, but we don't need to be

depressed. We may grieve for an appropriate time over genuine sorrows, but we're not to give up on life. Psalm 30 describes David's depression as being in the pit. Have you ever been down there with him? But notice what this discouraged king did. David cried unto God, "Thou hast healed me. . .thou hast lifted me up. . . thou hast brought up my soul from the grave; thou hast kept me alive. . .thou hast turned my mourning into dancing; thou hast put off my sackcloth and girded me with gladness. . . . Weeping may endure for a night, but *joy* cometh in the morning."

How blessed I have been by these verses! I may be weeping tonight, but when I ask for *joy*, it is mine in the morning!

Do you wake up full of fear? Is your blanket weighted down with worry? Are you too depressed to get up? Nehemiah 8:10 says, "The *joy* of the Lord is your strength!" Why not ask for it? You may have been weeping today, "but *joy* cometh in the morning."

Don't let your black cloud hover over you any longer. Ask God for a silver lining.

3. *Study God's Word.* As I searched the Bible for words of joy, I was encouraged by Jeremiah 15:16: "Thy words were found, and I did eat them, and thy word was unto me the *joy* and rejoicing of mine heart, for I am called by thy name." Jeremiah was a believer, called by God's name, and he was searching for contentment. What he found was God's words. He did not just glance at them; he did not put them away until he had time; he ate them. Jeremiah put God's words inside him and their digestion produced *joy*.

If we were to look at our depression as an overdrawn bank account, the preceding steps would have brought us up to zero. We would have gone from the minus column up to a break-even point. Once we decide we *need a change*, we are on our way. When we are willing to *face our depression as a sin* and *confess* this sin to God, we take a giant step. Once we *forget the past*, we make great progress; and when we *ask God to give us joy* and HE DOES, we break even.

Now that we have made this climb up to zero, we must put some reserves in the bank so we'll not be overdrawn again. Where does a Christian believer get the reserves? What can he fall back on? How can he keep the account full? Jeremiah turned to God's words and they brought him joy.

There is a never-ending supply of treasure in the Bible, but we must mine the nuggets for ourselves. The Bible will not run around after us; we have to seek to find. We can listen to good teachers and hear a sermon each week, but only when we study for ourselves do we begin to store up truths and verses that will help us in the present and in the future. "Thy word have I hid in my heart that I might not sin against thee" (Psalm 119:11).

When I began to study the Bible in earnest, God began to speak to me in a personal way. Soon I started teaching others the little I knew, and then I dug in deeper to stay ahead of my class. As I stored up God's Word in my heart, I grew as a Christian. I went up from zero and began to put reserves in my emotional bank. Now when I feel discouraged I know where to turn for help before it is too late. I have a full account to draw upon and my savings are secure.

Psalm 119:105 says, "Thy word is a lamp unto my feet." It lights my way. It brightens me. It gives me joy.

It is true that meditating on God's Word brings us joy, but unfortunately some depressed people don't want help. Recently I dealt with a lady from my Bible study who confessed, "I haven't opened my Bible in over a month."

I knew she was low and asked her why she wasn't reading her Bible.

"Because," she said, "I know if I study the Bible, I'll get over my depression."

She knew she was depressed and knew the Bible had the answers, but she wasn't ready for a cure. Many of us refuse to study God's Word when we are depressed because down deep we don't want to improve. Yet true happiness and joy come from God as He speaks to us through His Word.

When I was in Fresno, Frances told me of her aunt who was depressed. She lived alone, ate poorly, and was in bad health. She didn't care to live and she had simply taken to her bed hoping to die. When Frances found her aunt in this condition, she took her home to care for her. Each morning Frances read to her from the Psalms. At first the aunt didn't seem to hear, but after a few weeks she began to pay attention. Later she told Frances, "It was your reading the Bible that gave me the will to live. As I listened to David cry out to God, I cried out in my heart and God heard me."

Marion, a beautiful girl in the Norton Bible Study I used to teach, had reason to be depressed. She was divorced and her former husband had the children. She had to work hard to support herself and was often alone. Through our class she had become a dedicated Christian and came faithfully each week. One day she handed me this note:

> When depression comes over me it's a hopeless, lonely, isolated feeling. Self-pity just tears me up. Nobody cares, nothing will ever be good. If I sit with that mood the feeling

gets worse. I have to decide I don't want to continue feeling that way. I tell God He can have it—take it. The 23rd Psalm and other psalms always help. Pretty soon I remember things that need to be done. I thank the Lord and gain new confidence.

Marion had found that she must eat the Word of God to be uplifted. The joy of the Lord is her strength.

How much time do you spend a week in personal Bible study? It's great to be in study groups; it's even better to go off for weekend retreats; but until you sit down alone with God's Word before you, the thrill of firsthand messages from the Lord will remain a mystery to you.

4. *Write down your feelings.* "Do you know what I do when I'm depressed? I sit down and write out my feelings to the Lord." Lana had learned that putting it all down on paper relieved her depression. Once she expressed herself openly, she felt better.

Linda sent me a folder of poetry she had written during her depression, and it was beautiful. Each poem was a cry for help, and each conclusion showed the peace she received from the Lord.

Sometimes I've used writing as a purge for my problems. Once when we were in deep financial troubles and I couldn't see any way out, I wrote a letter to my children to explain our situation. As I wrote, verses of encouragement came to mind, and by the time I finished the letter I was uplifted. The Lord can use an open mind and a pen to cure as well as create.

David knew what depression was and composed music and verses to express his innermost feelings. In each psalm he first showed his grief and then shared his hope. Does David sound at all like you?

In Psalm 77:

> I cried unto God
> In the day of my trouble I sought the Lord.
> My soul refused to be comforted.
> I complained.
> My spirit was overwhelmed.
> Thou holdest mine eyes waking (insomnia).
> I am so troubled that I cannot speak.

In Psalm 55:

> Give ear to my prayer, O God.
> I mourn in my complaint and make a noise.
> My heart is sore pained within me.
> The terrors of death are fallen upon me.
> Fearfulness and trembling are come upon me.
> Horror hath overwhelmed me.

In Psalm 42:

> As the hart panteth after the water brooks, so
>   panteth my soul after thee, O God.
> My soul thirsteth for God.
> My tears have been my meat day and night.
> I pour out my soul in me.

How beautifully David presented his grief to the Lord! Have you sat down alone with a pencil and paper? With a piano? With a guitar? Have you tried putting your anguish into words and then giving it to the Lord?

After David stated his problems, he followed them with questions.

In Psalm 42:

> Why art thou cast down, O my soul?
> Why art thou disquieted within me?
> Why hast thou forgotten me?
> Why go I mourning because of oppression?

In Psalm 77:

> Will the Lord cast off forever?
> Will he be favorable no more?
> Is his mercy clean gone forever?
> Hath God forgotten to be gracious?

Have you ever asked such questions? Is His mercy clean gone forever? I've had all those feelings, but never put them into such effective phrases.

Before David asks for God's solutions, he sings out his own wishes. Do they sound like your desires?

> Oh, that I had wings like a dove! For then would I fly away and be at rest. Lo, then would I wander far off and remain in the wilderness. I would hasten my escape from the windy storm and tempest (Psalm 55:6-8).

How many women have said to me, "If only I could run away! If only I could escape!" Oh, for the wings of a dove that we might fly away! Human nature was the same for David as it is for us; the same God who watched over David is caring for us today. What a comfort!

As David cried to God in his despair, the Holy Spirit brought answers to David's mind. God gave him hope.

In Psalm 77:

I will remember the works of the Lord.
I will remember thy wonders of old.
I will meditate also of all thy work, and talk
    of thy doings.
Thou art the God that doest wonders.

God directed David: "Remember what I am able to do, David. Think about the miracles I've already performed in your life. Get your eyes off your problems, David, and meditate on me for a while. Stop reviewing your griefs with everyone who will listen and share what I've done for you. Be grateful, David; you have a God who does wonders!"

If you sat down and wrote to the Lord, He would answer you as He answered David. We have the same problems, the same God, and the same solutions.

In Psalm 55:

I will pray and cry aloud.
He shall hear my voice.
He hath delivered my soul in peace from the
    battle that was against me.
I will trust in thee.

God spoke to David: "When you pray and cry out to me, I hear you. When you trust in me, I give you peace." God gives those same conditions to you and to me.

In Psalm 42:

The Lord will command his lovingkindness in
    the daytime.
In the night his song shall be with me.
Hope thou in God, for I shall yet praise him,
    who is the health of my countenance and
    my God.

God reminded David: "My love is with you every day. When you wake at night, sing to me, for I am always there. You are not alone. And most important of all, David, remember that your *hope* is in me. When you praise me and trust me I will restore your mental health, and even your face will shine with joy!"

In our CLASS we teach a section on "journalizing," which is a word for a daily recording of our thoughts on paper. It is not a diary of events but a pouring out of our feelings, whether they are good or bad. As we encourage people to do this we are amazed at the letters of response we get. If you are interested in more information on journalizing and writing heartfelt letters to the Lord, read the chapter titled "Journalize for the Future" in the book *It Takes So Little To Be Above Average.*

Why not put your thoughts on paper in whatever form comes to your mind? Listen for God's answers and record them. Share your ideas with other people and send me a copy of what God has said through you so that I might use your words to encourage other people.

5. *Hope in God.* You may have lost hope in money; I have. You may have lost hope in government, schools, and medicine. You may have lost hope in your family, friends, and yourself, but remember: Hopelessness is the chief ingredient of depression.

As I write this section on hope today, I remember my son Larry. Through his 19 years of life he never grew. Larry couldn't see, hear, or think. Larry was hopeless. Once my hope for happiness was in Larry, but now Larry is dead and my hope for *joy*, in spite of adverse circumstances, is in God.

> People may disappoint us: Never worship people.

Money may disappear: Don't put your faith in
the dollar.
Houses may crumble: Don't idolize your
drapes.

When our hope is in things of the world and they
collapse, we become quickly depressed. When our
hope is in God, we can lose our possessions and yet
keep our minds.

Someone else is living in my dream house.
We no longer have the money we used to
enjoy.
We have produced two hopeless sons.

Yet God has blessed our home, our marriage, and our
ministry because we put our *hope* in God.

Thou wilt keep him in perfect peace whose
mind is stayed on thee, because he trusteth in
thee (Isaiah 26:3).

Can you really trust the Lord today? Is your mind
on yourself or on Him? Is He keeping you in perfect
peace?

You can know "the peace of God, which passes all
understanding and keeps your hearts and minds safe
in Christ Jesus" (Philippians 4:7).

SPIRITUAL INVENTORY

If you have doubts about whether you are a committed Christian, take a few moments to think it over. Can
you remember a specific time when you received the
Lord into your life? Do you pray daily for the power

of the Holy Spirit to work in your life? Is the Bible meaningful and exciting to you? Does the love of the Lord radiate from you? If you're not sure of your spiritual commitment, follow these steps that changed my life and pray these brief prayers with sincerity.

1. *Believe in Jesus.* "Lord Jesus, today I believe in You and ask You to come into my life. I agree with John 1:12 that when I believe in You and receive You into my heart, You will give me power and accept me into Your family. I need to know that I am accepted and belong to You. Thank You for keeping Your word. Amen."

2. *Give yourself away.* "Lord Jesus, today I give myself to You. I have not done as well with myself as I had hoped. I am discontented and unhappy. I am going to follow Romans 12:1,2. Right now I present my body to You—not just my soul, but all of me—for Your use. I give myself as a living sacrifice. From here on You direct and control me. Transform me into the kind of person You want me to be. Thank You for taking me in. I look forward to my new life in Christ. Amen."

3. *Don't be alone.* "Lord Jesus, I have often felt alone with my problems. I've not known where to turn, but You tell me in Matthew 28:20 that You are always with me. I want Your company. I need the assurance that You are at my side. Thank You, Lord, for being my Friend, for lifting me up so that I can bear my burdens. Amen."

4. *Desire a change.* "Lord Jesus, I have not been willing to improve. I have been waiting for my circumstances to change so I could be happy. I realize now that joy comes from the Lord, and I want to do all I can to live a positive Christian life. You tell us that You have come that we might have an abundant life, and I desire that change. Lord, make me willing to follow

Your directions for my life. I am assured by Philippians 2:13, 'God is always at work in you to make you willing and able to obey his own purpose' (TEV). Thank You. Amen.''

5. *Deal with guilt.* ''Lord Jesus, I have written down my list of guilts. I found I had done many things wrong and had neglected much I should have done. I ask You to move me in the right direction and clean up my guilts. I found I was carrying unnecessary guilts around. I give You those guilts today. Take them and give me the relief I need. I accept Your assurance that I can cast all my cares upon You, for You care for me (2 Peter 5:7). Thank You, Jesus. Amen.''

6. *Confess your sins.* ''Lord Jesus, in the eyes of the world I am not a sinner. I am a good person. Yet You say that all have sinned and come short of the glory of God (Romans 3:23). You tell me that 'to him who knoweth to do good and doeth it not, to him it is sin' (James 4:17). There has been much in my past where I knew to do good and didn't do it. I confess the following failures and sins and ask You to forgive me of

_____

_____

_____

Thank You for telling me that when I confess my sins to You, You will forgive me and cleanse me. I know now that I am forgiven. I know I am clean in Your sight. Thank You, Lord. Amen.''

7. *Forget the past.* ''Lord Jesus, I am burdened by my past mistakes. My daily actions are held down by the weights of yesterday. Lift these dark clouds from me, Lord, and make me forget the past. Clear up my mind so I can strive forward in Your will. With Paul I say, 'My single purpose in life is to forget what is

behind me and to reach for what is ahead.' Thank You for putting my focus in the right direction. Amen."

8. *Ask for joy.* "Lord Jesus, You don't want me depressed any longer. Even though my circumstances aren't right, I know You can give me joy. You want me to shine as a light in the world even in the midst of a crooked and perverse nation (Philippians 2:15). I don't have to wait for everything to get straightened out. I just have to ask You for joy, and I do, Lord. Lift my depression and pessimism and give me Your joy. Thank You, Lord. Amen."

9. *Study God's Word.* "Lord Jesus, I know I can't grow as a Christian unless I eat Your Word. I feed my body well but I neglect my spirit. I promise You now that I will begin to read the Bible. I know I can't be good at any subject until I have studied the text. I want to learn everything You have to say. I promise I will be a newborn babe desiring the sincere milk of the Word that I may grow thereby (1 Peter 2:2). Thank You for providing my spiritual food. Amen."

10. *Write down feelings.* "Lord Jesus, I have kept so much bottled up inside me. I have suppressed anger against those who have wronged me. I have envy for those who have done well. I have bitterness for those who have deceived me. Lord, my mind is a mess. If I write it all down, will You empty me of these burdens? If I am heavy-laden, will You give me rest? Lord, I am going to pour out my heart to You like David did. I am going to write down my feelings and give them all to You, for Your yoke is easy and Your burden is light. Hear me, O Lord. Amen."

11. *Hope in God.* "Lord Jesus, if it weren't for You I would have given up. I have been looking for that blessed hope and You have given it to me. If I had to depend on the world I would continue to despair, but

You have given me living hope. I pray with David: 'In thee, O Lord, do I put my trust . . . deliver me speedily, be thou my strong rock . . . pull me out of the net . . . for thou art my strength . . . set my feet in a large room . . . I am in trouble . . . mine eye is consumed with grief . . . I am forgotten as a dead man out of mind . . . I am like a broken vessel . . . make thy face to shine upon me.' Thank You for comforting me with the words, 'Be of good courage and he shall strengthen your heart, all ye that hope in the Lord.' Amen."

10

How to Live with a Depressed Person

How can we help others? Hopefully we now have a basic understanding of what depression is and a list of potential solutions. While a little knowledge can be a dangerous thing, it's better to have a limited grasp of the problem than none at all. At least we have somewhere to start.

It is always difficult to help a partner or relative because you are both preconditioned by your mutual past. The distressed person does not welcome advice from a mate and tends to see your good mental health as a barrier to communication. If someone in your family is seriously depressed, try to encourage him to get outside help. But in the interim here are some suggestions.

1. *Encourage him to talk about his feelings.* When a person is depressed he or she has a low self-image and a defeated attitude. Almost anything you say can exaggerate his concept of the problem. Even a compliment can be taken in a negative way.

He: Your hair looks lovely today.
She: What was wrong with it yesterday?

Understanding the touchy nature of the depressed, you should try to encourage them to talk. This conversation may not come easily.

He: What's the matter with you?
She: Nothing.
He: I mean why are you quiet?
She: I am not quiet.
He: I know there's something wrong.
She: There's nothing wrong. I just want to be quiet.

With a script like this, anyone could lose his cool, but patience is a must if we are to help a depressed person. Drop the subject and try again another day.

Before Fred dedicated his life to the Lord Jesus, he was often depressed. At that point I knew nothing about the subject except that I didn't like his moods. I would ask him what was bothering him and he would deny he had a problem. He hardly spoke, and when he did he was very polite. "Please pass the salt. Thank you very much." The more depressed, the more polite.

After a week or two of this meaningless but mannered conversation, I was ready to scream, "What is the matter with you, you dummy?" In fact, sometimes I did. Eventually he would tell me about some cute statement I had made last July that had hurt him.

I would then yell, "Is that all? For that you've been a deaf-mute for months?"

These loving and logical questions would devastate him and he would sink into a worse depression. Now I at least knew what was bothering him and I could explain to my friends, as Fred sat there like a statue of Moses, "You'll *never* believe what he's upset about *this* time!"

Does that scene sound familiar to you? So many men and women have told me similar stories. Those of us who aren't depressed beg the victim to tell us his troubles, but when he does we scream in disbelief. We condemn him and he decides, "I will never tell her anything again." And he doesn't.

To help a depressed person we must ask repeatedly until he responds, and then say, "I understand. I would feel the same way in your position."

Once you accept his concern as genuine, you remove the barrier and he dares to talk. As you converse, listen for genuine clues, agree that he has a problem, and share loving hope for the future.

2. *Don't try to jolly him up.* An inexperienced partner will try to jolly up his mate. "It's a beautiful day. Let's all be happy." "Cheer up, Honey. Things are never as bad as they look."

When Fred became depressed, I got hopefully enthusiastic. "Come on, Fred. Be bright like me!" The brighter I got, the duller he became. Finally I learned: Fred felt he was in a deep hole, alone and helpless. When I looked down and dropped cheer upon him, it turned to rain. As he saw me standing over him bouncing with joy, his self-image sank to zero. I couldn't help Fred while I was running around in the sunshine. I had to go quietly down into the pit and join him. Once we were both on an even level, we could begin to climb up together.

"I know where you are, Fred. I'm with you. I understand your problem and we're going to conquer this together."

The depressed person needs a loving, understanding mate, not a cheerleader.

3. *Remove any obvious pressures and worries.* Women, when your husband is depressed, it may be that he has insurmountable business problems. He may come home exhausted and hopeless. The last thing he needs at a time like this is a shrieking shrew with a list of complaints in her hand.

When your husband is under pressure at work, try to give him peace at home. Save the orthodontist's estimate until morning. Let the faucet drip another day.

Men, accept your wife's worries as real to her even if you think they're foolish. Listen all the way through to her resume of calamities and try to deal lovingly with each one in order. Help her discipline the children and never say, "The kids are *your* problem."

Don't point out, "Half these things would never have happened if you'd listened to me in the first place." When a woman is downhearted, she doesn't need a review of her faults; she needs help.

4. *Plan interesting events.* Since depressed people often see no joy ahead, they need some anticipated change of scene. Women: Plan a quiet dinner for two each Friday night. Let your husband know that the children will be away and that he can select the menu. Give him something relaxing to look forward to. Fred has often said to me, "I can take the pressures of business all week when I know you'll make my weekends pleasant."

Men: Think of something your wife would like to do, and then plan it. Don't ask if she wants to go away for a few days—just make the reservations. A change of scene can often give a new perspective to an old depression.

5. *Don't complain.* One sure way to perpetuate a

depression is to point out each fault as you find it. Since the victim already feels worthless, constant criticism is like a hammer pounding him into the floor.

Women, do you say:

Why don't you ever take me anywhere?
Why don't you get a decent job like Joe?
Why don't we have a Mercedes like the Smiths?
When are you going to fix the screen door?
Do you have to watch football all the time?
What's your excuse for being late tonight?
Don't you listen to anything I say?
Can't you ever smile, you old sourpuss?

Men, do you say:

Why don't you cook like my mother?
Why don't you look like Raquel Welch in a bathing suit?
Why isn't dinner ever on time?
Beef stew again?
Did you spend all day on the phone?
Do you know you're raising a bunch of bums?
Why is my chair always full of laundry?
Don't you have a brain in your head?

No one likes insults and complaints, but to a depressed person they come as a death knell. Always praise the accomplishments and overlook the failures.

6. *Don't get discouraged.* Living with a depressed person is no fun, but don't let it get you down. Spend as much time as you can with your partner, but don't let his gloom ruin you. Invite him to go places and encourage his participation, but if he refuses, don't feel guilty.

The depressed person is full of guilt and easily

transfers this feeling to other people. By his expressions and sighs he can make your conscience twinge. When you have done all you can to help the distressed person, rest in peace.

Gail's mother was extremely depressed. Gail had visited her each day, talked with her on the phone, bought her presents, and taken her to luncheons and Bible studies. Gail had done everything she could, but her mother always needed more. When we discussed the situation, Gail was full of guilt. "I know she's going to kill herself and I don't know what else to do. I can't even talk with her without getting depressed myself."

I questioned Gail carefully and determined that she had done everything possible for her mother. She was carrying unnecessary guilt and she had to get rid of it. We prayed together and she released her guilt to the Lord. A few months later I received this letter from Gail's sister:

> Dear Mrs. Littauer,
>
> I have just finished listening to your tape "Depression," and I'd like to share with you how much I enjoyed it.
>
> In April of this year, my sister Gail attended your conference in Phoenix, Arizona. After your lesson on depression, she talked with you because she saw that our mother was on number 16 or 17 of the symptom list. Without a doubt, her going to the conference and speaking to you personally was a direct leading from the Lord. At that point they were not speaking to each other because every time they had contact, Gail would be in a state of depression for days.
>
> Anyway, you talked to her and explained

that probably suicide was next, and also convinced her that if and when it did happen, she had no reason to have guilty feelings about it. (Gail often felt guilty about not having more compassion for her and wondered if she was a bad daughter.) So she ordered your tape on depression, and when it came she sent it to Mom. But Mom immediately sent it back without listening to it. That was the first of June. On June 26 Mom died of an overdose. She had talked about suicide, and actually attempted it before, but never took enough to do any real damage, so when it did happen, we were all pretty shocked.

When I went home for the funeral I was amazed. The peace Gail had was tremendous! And yet I expected her to take it the hardest because she lived in the same town, and because they had not been getting along. But through the conference God had prepared her for the end result. How I wish we'd all gone to the conference, especially Mom! But she didn't, and that can't be changed now. However, she was a born-again Christian, so I know she is with Jesus right now.

Again let me say thank you for talking to my sister. What a difference in the way she handled Mom's death! I know Jesus was leading both of you that day, and I praise God for Christians that are obedient to His directions.

Don't let a depressed friend or relative get you down. Do the best you can to provide solutions and then don't feel guilty. Remember: God holds you accountable for your own actions but not for their reactions.

11

How to Counsel
a Depressed Person

I never set out to counsel depressed women, yet I
see them every day. I never hung out a sign saying
"Depression Consultant," yet women find me. If there
are women in need everywhere I go, then you may
know a few. If you teach a Bible study, lead a discussion group, chair a committee, or marry a minister, you
may find yourself in demand as an instant counselor.
You may have no more idea of how to approach a
troubled person than I did when I first began, but I have
learned a lot and I want to share this growth with you.

We should never consider dealing with a seriously
disturbed person, but we may be of help to a confused
lady who is sinking and sees no one around but us to
save her. This chapter is specifically written for anyone
who may be in a position where people seek your
advice. I do not intend to train troops of little ladies
who will become overnight psychologists and run
around looking for clients. I only want to guide those
of you who are already beleaguered by a bevy of
troubled women and don't know what to do with

them. If you find yourself in this position, read on.

Counseling brings awesome responsibility. We must realize that we are dealing with real people who, with our advice, may try to change their whole direction in life. We cannot lightly drop heavy thoughts on weak people. For this reason I am making the following suggestions to those of you who may be faced with a counseling situation. I will use depression for my examples, but the principles will apply for any counseling problem.

1. *Know your subject.* Don't be guilty of counseling from ignorance. If you are going to be talking with depressed people, study everything you can find on the subject. Read this book several times until you feel you have mastered the subject. Be alert to helpful articles on depression, stress, and self-image, and keep up-to-date.

Every time I stand in a supermarket line I use the time to advantage. I skim over the topics on the magazine covers and pick up those which relate to my areas of study. I glance through the article. If it offers anything helpful, I buy it. Every time I sit down at home to read anything, I have a pencil in my hand and I underline pertinent material. I rip out all articles and file them under headings that I might need in the future.

Go to bookstores and the library and pick out appropriate books. Saturate yourself with the subject so that you will know more than you think you'll ever need. Don't expect to be an overnight expert, but if you follow these steps you will have a much bigger reservoir of knowledge next year than you have now.

My book *Lives on the Mend* will be an excellent source for any of you who counsel. It gives the case histories of 15 different women with problems and the way they overcame their difficulties. The subjects covered are alcoholism, drug addiction, phobias, adultery, divorce, single parenting, family stress, attempted murder, rape, incest, teen suicide, death of a child, handling grief, physical pain, and pains of the past. In each case we tell what people did that helped the person involved and what other people did that hurt. From the year I spent on the research and personal interviews for these topics, I have composed both life stories of real people and insightful instructions in dealing with these traumas of life.

For those of you who wish to counsel from the Bible, the perfect psychology manual, you must first read it. There are too many women doling out Scriptural directives who have no depth in the Word. Before you give out, you need to take in. Study as often as possible with the clear purpose of discovering the basic principles of correct living. I've done this for many years. I underline every verse that applies to marriage, depression, child-raising, counseling, women, responsibility, discipline, etc. I circle key words and index them for quick future reference.

To counsel from the Bible you must know what it says about life and where to find it. God's principles are true, consistent, and practical. Without them I couldn't counsel, speak, or teach. Even atheists can improve their lives by proper biblical application. But dedicated Christian believers are guaranteed supernatural power when they are willing to follow God's plan for disciplined living.

Jay Adams' *The Christian Counselor's New Testament* indexes the places in the Bible where the current topics needed by a counselor are found.

Paul tells us: "All scripture is given by inspiration of God, and is profitable for doctrine, for reproof, for correction, for instruction in righteousness'' (2 Timothy 3:16).

Scripture is extremely useful for teaching and correcting, but we must know more than the 23rd Psalm if we are to apply the Word to our lives and to the lives of other people.

Ask God to open your eyes to the truths He has for your use and then ''study to show thyself approved unto God, a workman that needeth not to be ashamed, rightly dividing the word of truth'' (2 Timothy 2:15). Be careful about using Scripture to condemn or instill guilt. Too often Christians use God's Word to judge the sins of other people. Before you give out verses, ask yourself whether this is how Jesus would use Scripture. Are you rightly dividing the Word of truth?

Jay Adams' *The Christian Counselor's New Testament* indexes the places in the Bible where the current topics needed by a counselor are found.

2. *Beware of friends.* Many years ago I had a lovely friend with a lot of problems. As we lunched together she would often share her problems with me in detail. One day after I offered some obvious advice, she relayed it to her husband, who was affronted with my bold suggestions. By the time she reported this, they were both upset with me. The advice was sound, but it had come from a friend, and I realized that I could be either her friend or her counselor, but not both. We decided to be friends, and she went to another counselor whose advice would not be taken personally.

To be of use to another person, we must speak plainly, pointing out the real problem and alternative solutions. When the receiver is a friend, we are hampered in giving an honest appraisal and tend to agree with their often one-sided and distorted view.

When I counsel seriously, I sometimes have to be

blunt. This hurts, but it saves time and puts the issue clearly on the line. I once had some women say to me, "I didn't like what you said, but it was right." They had already asked friends who had agreed, "Yes, your husband is a rat." It is easy to gather support for one's own selfish and rebellious attitudes, but a good counselor has to speak the truth in love as well as to listen.

3. *Establish desire.* When I began to counsel, I listened to women's problems by the hour. I heard the description of every fight, every heartache, and every misunderstanding. One day after a lengthy recital of woes from a Christian worker, I talked with Dr. Henry Brandt about the amount of time I was spending with each person. He told me directly, "The first thing you have to establish in counseling is whether the person wants help or an audience. Some women are professional counsel-seekers telling their troubles to everyone who will listen. Learn to sort them out."

From that point on I found ways of establishing the desire of the person in need. The simplest way is to ask, after an appropriate time of listening, "Are you interested in doing something about this problem?"

Possible answers:

Like what?
I guess so.
It's really his fault.
I've already done all I can.
What else do you expect of me?

Translation:

If it's really easy.
Not if I can help it.

Not till he shapes up.
No way!
You've got to be crazy.

These answers show a lack of any resolve to get to the bottom of the problem.
Sometimes I ask:

"Suzy, have you talked this over with anyone else before?"
"Yes, I went to Pastor Jones."
"What did he tell you to do?"
"He said I should stay home and clean the house and be pleasant to my husband."
"Have you done this?"
"Well, not yet."
"When did he suggest this?"
"Last summer."

If Suzy has not yet acted on the counsel she was given last summer, you have a clue that Suzy doesn't really want an answer.

Another indication comes when the person seeking counsel becomes defensive.

"Well, what do *you* expect of me?"
"There's *no way* that would work."
"You want *me* to change *my* attitude?"
"Well, that's ridiculous!"

Margaret came to me recently. She gets depressed every summer because the kids are home and everything is out of control. She is also furious at her husband because he wants her to drop everything and go to company banquets with him.

When I suggested how she might organize her household, she countered each plan with an adamant reason why it would never work. I tried to deal with the anger she had for her husband and found that she was even more defensive. I told her she should be grateful that her husband wanted to take her out, and she countered with, "Do you mean to tell me *you* want *me* to go to those crummy banquets?" Suddenly the banquets were my fault. Counseling is not a fun-filled hobby, and we should not tie up our time with people who do not have a teachable attitude.

I once referred a deeply rebellious woman to Dr. Brandt. He quickly discovered that she didn't want an answer, and within ten minutes he had sent her on her way. He told her that when she *really* wanted help, he would be glad to talk with her. She called me up and yelled at me for suggesting him. I listened and apologized. A few days later she phoned again. She had decided she did need counsel and had gone back to Dr. Brandt. This time she listened! "I went to a lot of people for help," she said, "but he's the first one who told me I didn't really want advice. I was furious, but he was right."

Until the person is willing to admit he has a need and accepts the fact that *he* must do something about it, the greatest counsel in the world is a waste of time.

Let us assume that you have done your homework on depression and are dealing with a non-friend who truly wants help. She is a sweet girl but is depressed. You explain that depression is a common problem, but there is hope: "Together we'll come to a helpful solution."

4. *Examine the past, present, and future.* It's important to establish a warm relationship and let her know that you and she are going to work together on

this. Don't set an attitude of "I am the big perfect counselor and you are the mixed-up dummy." She already feels insecure and needs assurance that you care and there is hope.

You ask her, "What is your problem?" and then listen for as long as it takes for you to grasp the situation. Ask any questions necessary to fill in your gaps, but don't prolong the story by asking for inconsequential details. As she talks, you will begin to see consistent actions and reactions. It is your job to:

Find the real problem.

You are dealing with her *past* and finding out what the problem is and how she got into this situation.

Guide her in selecting the best alternative.

You are acting on the *present* by discussing what she can do about the problem.

Bring about changes in her established behavior pattern.

You are planning the *future* by showing her how to change her lifestyle so she won't get into these troubles again.

Find the real problem. Do not be fooled into thinking that the stated problem is necessarily the real problem. Listen well, and as you play detective the real villain will appear.

Ingrid asked, "I am tormented by a Scriptural question: Do unborn babies have souls?"

"Did you have an abortion?" I asked.

"How did you know?"

Alice said, "I'm depressed and can't sleep nights." I asked, "Do you have a guilty conscience?"

She burst into tears. "I'm driving around afternoons with a traveling salesman and I'm scared to death I'll get caught."

With practice you will soon be able to get to the heart of the real problem and not waste time treating some symptom.

Some counselors spend years on the past. I listen only enough to give me an understanding of the situation and then pick up with the here-and-now. Most people with problems love to review the past. They want to make an epic movie of their adventures, and some are worth it, but if you want to accomplish something in the *present*, cut off the *past* as soon as you feel you have enough information.

Guide her in selecting the best alternative. In dealing with the *present* there has to be an acceptance of the fact: This is where I am today. What am I going to do about it now?

People are uncomfortable with today and want to slip back into the murky past. It's your job to keep them on current events, not history, unless their problems stem from childhood pain.

You must help your counselee bring out all the possible alternative solutions to her problem and list them in her writing. Once you both look at them, the worst ones will become absurd. And as you discuss the probable consequences of each alternative, let her choose which is best. Depressed people resist making decisions and want you to tell them what to do so that when they mishandle the action they can blame it on poor counsel. *Do not make their decisions.* Steer them into the correct choice by reviewing the consequences and then congratulate them for their decision. Mention several times, "*You* have made a good choice."

This repetition does two things: It relieves you of future responsibility and it shows them that they can make a decision.

Unfortunately, many amateur counselors love to make impressive commandments to the poor soul seated before them and enjoy the power they seem to exercise over this individual.

Many such women come from unpleasant home situations, and straightening out other people in worse shape than they are becomes their hobby.

If you are doing any type of counseling, don't flaunt your wisdom. This is not a glory job; it is a humble opportunity to help a distressed person. Your responsibility is not to be brilliant, but to guide a person in need into making a proper decision. Sometimes the best thing you can do is to get the individual to a counselor who can properly handle the problem.

One other important point in counseling is to keep your mouth shut. Knowing the dingy background of some poor lady inspires us to tell others about her. Those we tell are pledged to secrecy, but sometimes our words return to the source. A friend of mine went to a local pastor and poured out a lurid tale about her daughter. She begged him not to say a word to anyone, especially his secretary. The minute she left, he told his secretary the whole story and the secretary called me. I was aghast at my friend's heartbreaking problem, and before I hung up the phone my friend was at the door. She told me what had happened and I had to be surprised for a second time.

When anyone comes to us with a personal problem we must keep it strictly confidential. Don't think you are doing the girl a favor by sharing her needs at prayer meeting. I once was at a study group where a pastor's wife asked us to pray for Agnes' daughter who was being sent out of town for six months.

Remember, you lose your credibility and effectiveness when you share tales with other people. Don't say anything you wouldn't want Agnes to overhear.

Bring about changes in her established behavior pattern. Much informal counseling stops with the *present*. "If you do this today, you will be fine." But to leave the *past* and the *present* standing alone is like putting a Band-Aid over the problem: It gives only temporary relief. If the *past* gets us into trouble, and the *present* handles it, what will happen in the *future*? We cannot let the person think that today's isolated act is the answer. There must be an evaluation of the pattern of the *past* and a desire to change *future* behavior as well.

Tom, a businessman, came to me. His wife was going to leave him and he was depressed. She wanted financial security, and he was going to get it for her someday if she would only be patient.

PAST:

> Tom had been in many different businesses. They all were going to make a fortune. He had charm and could always get backers for his deals. Bad luck followed him and each venture collapsed, leaving debts and broken friendships. He meant well and he was sure to do better someday if she would only wait.

PRESENT:

> Current business is in trouble.

Alternatives:
1. Go bankrupt again.
2. Sell the business.
3. Stop playing around and get to work.

In discussion we concluded that his wife would be most upset by number 1, although it was the easy way. She had been humiliated when he left friends holding the bag before, and she was sure to leave him if he went bankrupt again. He canceled out number 1.

He would sell the business. He had an offer, but it wasn't big enough to make a profit. I pointed out how grateful he should be that anyone would want such a shaky business. "I never thought of it that way," he replied.

Part of the reason he had a failing business was that he was too busy playing golf with "important people" and planning future schemes.

Do you see the pattern here? The stated problem is: My wife is going to leave me even though I'm trying to make money for her. The real problem is: Tom is a charming bum who really doesn't want to grow up and be a responsible adult.

His *past* shows repeated attempts to strike it rich without proper follow-through. When his dreams fail he ditches them, along with his friends' money, and tries again. He has no idea what it means to be responsible. His wife is not his problem; he is.

His *present* choice was to sell his business, pay off his obligations, and get a job where he could do the front work and someone else the follow-up.

His *future* depended upon his willingness to confess his failures, assess his talents, get to work, and become a mature husband. He had to understand that he was unsuited to run a business and that until he grew up he needed to work in a disciplined organization where he was held accountable for his performance.

It's not easy to share these blunt facts with a man, but to do any less would only encourage his indolence and immaturity.

DEPRESSION QUESTIONNAIRE

Name_____Date_____

PAST

1. Find the *real* problem:

   Apparent problem _____

   _____

   Real problem _____

   _____

2. Examine the background:

   Born loser   _____
   Successful   _____
   Can't communicate   _____
   Can't compete   _____
   Too much to do   _____
   Nothing to do   _____
   Drastic circumstances   _____
   Serious illness   _____
   Low self-image   _____
   Too high standards   _____
   Feeling guilty   _____
   Other problems   _____

3. Check the symptoms:
   Passiveness   _____

Loss of interest   _____
Pessimism   _____
Hopelessness   _____
Self-deprecation   _____
Withdrawal   _____
Preoccupation with self   _____
Dislike of happy people   _____
Change of personality   _____
Fatigue   _____
Insomnia   _____
Overeating   _____
Undereating   _____
Increase in drinking   _____
Drug-taking   _____
Poor concentration   _____
Hypochondria   _____
Suicidal tendencies   _____
Sudden improvement   _____
Call to death   _____

PRESENT

1. List the alternatives:

   _____
   _____
   _____

2. Review the consequences:

   _____
   _____
   _____

3. State their decision:

   _____
   _____

FUTURE

1. Analyze faulty behavior patterns:
   _____
   _____
   _____

2. Plan future corrections:
   _____
   _____
   _____

3. Establish needed goals:
   _____
   _____
   _____

Possible health problems:
_____
_____

Assignment:
_____
_____
_____

Suggested help:

Books _____
Tapes _____
Counselors _____
Agencies _____

5. *Use the Depression Questionnaire.* To help you counsel in an organized and productive manner, I have

included the preceding questionnaire which will put the problem on paper where you can see it. It's so easy to spend an hour with a distressed person and get nowhere. It is difficult to pull together all the facts of the case and come up with a workable solution. I hope this chart will bring an overwhelming job into a possible range.

You can use this questionnaire while you're with the individual, or have him fill it out afterward. Since the majority of depressed people are introspective and analytical, I find that they like to work on the chart with me and then take it home to study. I file my copy of the questionnaire for future reference and return visits.

Dividing the discussion into past, present, and future gives you an easy-to-remember outline. It will be even easier to counsel if you run off a few copies of the questionnaire.

PAST

Find the real problem. We have already examined the need for getting to the heart of the problem. You ask for the person's opinion and then sift through the scenario for the real problem. When you feel you have found the truth, ask lovingly, "Could this possibly be part of your problem?"

Don't be shocked with a vehement denial. I have found that the more a person resists the real cause, the closer I have come. I then pull back and say, "I'm sorry. It just seemed to make sense to me."

Invariably by the end of the session or by the next day the person says, "Maybe what you mentioned is right." The seed is planted, and if it's correct he or she will usually pick up on it later. When you both agree on the real problem, write it down.

Examine the background. In order to use this checklist effectively, you must first study Chapter 4, "Who Gets Depressed?" As depressed people tell you their stories, you can usually see quickly what their past has been.

The *born loser* will say, "My mother told me I'd never amount to much."

The *successful person* who's depressed says, "I've always been able to handle everything. I can't figure out what's wrong with me."

Those who *can't communicate* will have great difficulty stating their case.

Those who *can't compete* will want you to decide everything.

Those with *too much to do* will try to impress you with the community's need for their services and will list all their activities. They will want an instant solution that won't involve much time on their part.

Those with *nothing to do* will be lonely and bored. They need a friend.

Those in *drastic circumstances* will tell you about it: death, divorce, moving, job loss, son on drugs, serious illness.

Those with *low self-image* sometimes hide it under lovely clothes and false eyelashes. They often work at looking good to cover their insecurities.

Those with *too high standards* will tell you how disappointed they are that they have failed after trying so hard to make life perfect.

Those who are *feeling guilty* often express how weighted down they feel, and you have to discover whether the guilt is justified or unnecessary and deal with it correctly.

There may be many *other problems* that the past has

put upon this person. As they are exposed, write them down.

Once you have examined the background, you as a counselor will have an understanding of why this particular person has been depressed by this problem. Obviously the people with *too much to do* or *too little to do* will respond to different solutions. Knowing where the person has come from will keep you from heading in the wrong direction.

Check the symptoms. Before deciding where a person sits on the scale of symptoms, reread Chapter 3. Imagine that you are talking with a depressed lady. Ask some questions to establish the depth of her depression. Do not exclaim, "Oh, this is terrible! You are already on step 10!"

Even though she doesn't know that her constant exhaustion is step 10, she will, at your proclamation, immediately drop lower. Instead say, "I talk with many people who are at the same point you are, but there is always a reason and we'll find it."

This depressed lady doesn't need to know how far down she is but rather how far up she can go. If you find that she is in the suicidal range, you must get professional help. Don't take it upon yourself to deal with a person on the brink of suicide—the consequences can be devastating for both of you.

By the time you have reviewed the *past*, you probably have a good picture of the person and the problem. Now what are you going to do about it in the *present*?

PRESENT

List the alternatives and review the consequences. Never let the person leave you the first time without a glimmer of hope. He must see that there are some possibilities. Ask, "What are your alternatives?" When he hesitates, I suggest the first choice: Do nothing.

This startles the person, who usually replies, "If I didn't want to do anything I wouldn't have come to you."

This is a natural response and is actually a commitment to action, so congratulate him: "I'm so glad you want to do something. What are the possibilities?"

Don't be surprised when depressed people don't have any immediately. That's why they've come to you; they see no way out. Help them to put something down on paper.

Thirty-two-year-old Sharon came to me bored and disturbed. Her *past* had been wonderful. She had been an airline stewardess and lived a glamorous life. At *present* she had a spacious house, two little daughters, and a husband who traveled. She resented his trips because she had to stay home. "He has all the fun."

To punish him she did very little housework and gained weight. She often reminded her husband and children how they had ruined her life. "I think they ought to know I really was important before I got tied down with them," she said proudly.

Her stated reason for depression: Her husband travels and her life is dull. The real problem: Sharon is a self-centered person who prefers to live in the *past* and refuses to grow up and accept her *present* role as a wife and mother.

When I asked her for alternatives she said quickly, "He should get a different job." We wrote that down as number 1 and then looked at the consequences. He makes a big salary plus commission on his present job. His territory is secure and he knows his clients well. Sharon likes her big house and the membership in the country club. A new job might mean less money, and she is not willing to risk this loss.

I showed her alternative 1: He should get a different job. Then we weighed the consequences: She might have to change her lifestyle. When I made this point clear she said, "I'd be stupid to want to go backward."

"Then we have to eliminate number 1," I said.

"But I want him to change."

"But *you* don't want to change. You just want to complain."

"I never thought of it that way," she said.

Sharon did not want her *own* first choice when she saw that it might mean sacrifice from her.

I suggested a pleasant alternative: Get a sitter and go with him on a few trips. She told me immediately that he didn't want her to go. As I dug into this, she admitted he had invited her frequently but she had refused under the guise of being a devoted mother. Since I knew that in Sharon's case motherhood was not a valid deterrent to pleasure, I probed further. Finally the real reason came out: She was ashamed of her looks and didn't want his clients to see the former stewardess gone frumpy.

No wonder Sharon was depressed! She was angry at her husband who had all the fun and was worn out from self-deception. It was much easier to live in the *past* than do something about the *present*. It was so much easier to blame a good man, making an exceptional living and inviting her to travel with him, than it was to look at herself and shape up.

Sharon chose alternative 3: Face reality and grow up. The consequences were that she lost weight, became a better mother, and no longer heaped guilt on the children for her failures. At first she didn't agree with my suggestion to apologize to her children for her past behavior. One day she called to tell me she had told her girls she was sorry for being a grumpy mother. Afterward one daughter looked up and said, "You mean it wasn't our fault you were unhappy?"

When the objective counsel of a willing person is acted upon, whole families can be changed. Help those in need. *List the alternatives. Review the consequences.* Then guide them into making a life-changing decision.

FUTURE

According to the complexity of the problem, you may need to postpone planning the *future* until you see the person acting upon the *present*. Whenever the time is right, help him to look ahead. Even if the current crisis is patched up, problems may reoccur if there is not an inner change of attitude.

Sharon can lose weight and clean house, but unless she gets rid of her anger at her husband it will crop up again. Unless she really loves her children, they will sense her resentment. It is easier to shed pounds than guilt. It is easier to clean up a house than a mind.

Humanly speaking it's almost impossible to change an established pattern of behavior, but the Bible tells us we can *be transformed* and *receive a new mind*; we can *know* what is the good, acceptable, and perfect *will of God for us* (Romans 12:1,2).

Secular counseling can ferret out the *past*; it can even give practical answers for the *present*; but it has never found the power to change the *future*.

John is an alcoholic doctor. He is losing his practice and is depressed. He went to a counselor who told him he drank to cover up his fear of failure. He is afraid he will lose a patient in surgery. The more he fears, the more he drinks, and the less competent he becomes. That's the *past*. The *present* demands that he quit drinking immediately. Alcoholics Anonymous knows that there is no hope without belief in a higher power. An affected person can't do it on his own; he needs divine help.

It's in the area of future change of established patterns that the Christian counselor has the answer. No matter how sincere a person may be, he cannot change his inner attitudes alone. He can vent his anger, kick pillows, and get it all out, but the spirit of anger is still inside him, building up for the next explosion. Our own strong wills and positive thinking can help us today, but we need spiritual power to bring about permanent change in our personal habit patterns. "Except the Lord build the house, they labor in vain that build it" (Psalm 127:1).

If you are planning to help other people with their problems, make sure you are a committed believer yourself. If you doubt your spiritual rebirth, go back to the Spiritual Inventory at the end of Chapter 9.

The Lord Jesus Himself told the believers He had a gift for them: "You shall receive power when the Holy Spirit has come upon you" (Acts 1:8 NKJV).

Without me you can do nothing (John 15:5).

Our sufficiency is of God (2 Corinthians 3:5).

Good does not live in me. . . . For even though the desire to do good is in me, I am not able to do it (Romans 7:18 TEV).

But truly I am full of power by the Spirit of the Lord (Micah 3:8).

God anointed Jesus of Nazareth with the Holy Spirit and with power (Acts 10:38).

> God hath power to help (2 Chronicles 25:8).

> Power belongeth unto God (Psalm 62:11).

> Jesus beheld them and said unto them, "With men this is impossible, but with God all things are possible" (Matthew 19:26).

With these verses of power at the very center of your being you can share with weary people the message of hope in Jesus Christ. You can assure everyone that—

> He who hath the Son hath life (1 John 5:12).

Then make sure they have the Son. You can give them Jesus' assurance:

> I am the way, the truth, and the life. No man cometh unto the Father but by me (John 14:6).

When you have established a base of spiritual communication with a person, you can begin to work toward a hopeful future. While it is important to put out today's fires, it is also imperative to prevent them from flaring up again in the future.

Paul gives us guidelines for Christian counseling in Ephesians:

> Through Jesus Christ [God made] us his sons—this was his pleasure and purpose (1:5 TEV).

> You heard the true message, the Good News that brought you salvation. You believed in

Christ, and God put his stamp of ownership upon you by giving you the Holy Spirit he had promised (1:13 TEV).

In chapter 2 Paul assures us:

You are now fellow citizens with God's people and members of the family of God (2:19 TEV).

In chapter 3 he asks God—

To give you power through his Spirit to be strong in your inner selves and. . .that Christ will make his home in your hearts through faith. . .that you. . .may have the power to understand how broad and long, how high and deep, is Christ's love (3:16-18 TEV).

In chapter 4 he tells us to—

Grow up in every way to Christ, who is the head (4:15 TEV).

To become mature people, reaching to the very height of Christ's full stature (4:13 TEV).

If we stop here for a moment, we can see that Paul has laid out the basics for Christian counseling. Make sure your subject is a Christian. Make sure he knows he is God's son (through Jesus Christ). Assure him of the power of the Holy Spirit in his life now that he is in God's family. Show him he will be strong in his inner self with Christ at home in his heart and that he can know Christ's abundant love.

When he understands his place in the family, he must realize that it's time to grow up, face reality, and get on with life. He must throw away childish things and become a mature man. Many depressed people want to remain babies. It is easier to depend on other people for everything or blame others for their situation than it is to step out into the big world and make responsible decisions. Until the need for maturity is established, it is difficult to change behavior. A person must get out of the dream world, accept the situation as it is (not as he wishes it were), and move on from there. If you can get this far with a person, you can then bring his behavior patterns under the guidance of Scripture.

Paul tells us there is no hope for improvement until we are willing to throw away our old behavior and get rid of the patterns of the past that made us live as we used to. "Your hearts and minds must be made completely new, and you must put on the new self, which is created in God's likeness" (4:23,24 TEV).

Note how Paul says we *must* throw away the old behavior patterns that got us into this problem in the first place. Then, in case we can't figure out what's wrong with us, he gives us a checklist.

> *No more lying, then. Everyone must tell the truth* (4:25 TEV).
> How many women have spun webs of deception and are afraid they will get caught?

> *Do not let your anger lead you into sin, and do not stay angry all day* (4:26 TEV).

How many have anger poised on their lips, ready to explode?

Stop robbing and start working, in order to earn an honest living. . .and. . .help the poor (4:28 TEV).
How many mothers ask their children to watch for cops so they can speed? How many are lazy housewives nagging their husbands to earn more for them—not for the poor? How many men are involved in dishonest business arrangements?

Do not use harmful words, but only helpful words, the kind that build up and provide what is needed, so that what you say will do good to those who hear you (4:29 TEV).
How many women insult and degrade their husbands? How many men correct and direct their wives?

Do not make God's Holy Spirit sad (4:30 TEV).
How many understand that the Holy Spirit grieves over selfish acts?

Get rid of all bitterness, passion, and anger (4:31 TEV).
How many women are bitter and angry with their ex-husbands and turn children against their own fathers? How many men are still angry at their mothers and take it out on their wives?

No more shouting or insults (4:31 TEV).

How many men and women scream at their children and at each other and insult their in-laws?

No more hateful feelings of any sort (4:31 TEV).
How many store up hatred and harden their expressions?

Be kind and tenderhearted to one another (4:32 TEV).
How many exhibit a genuine Christian kindness and tenderhearted attitude to all?

Forgive one another, as God has forgiven you through Christ (4:32 TEV).
How many of us need to forgive one another and forget the wrongs, as Christ forgave us?

Do not be immoral, indecent, or greedy (5:3).
How many of us are doing immoral, indecent acts, hoping we won't be discovered? How many of us are greedy, wanting everything we see?

Do not use obscene, foolish, or dirty words (5:4).
How many men swear and tell dirty stories to be a macho man of the world?

Try to learn what pleases the Lord (5:10 TEV).
How many of us try to learn what pleases the Lord?

*Don't be fools. . .but try to find out what
the Lord wants you to do* (5:17 TEV).
How many of us are fools going our own
way and doing our own thing?

*Do not get drunk. . .which will only ruin
you; instead be filled with the Spirit* (5:18
TEV).
How many of us have tried to escape the
harsh reality of life by drinking ourselves
into oblivion, only to return depressed?

*Speak to one another in words of the
Psalms with praise in your hearts* (5:19).
How few of us can say in any situation,
"Praise the Lord anyhow"?

*Always give thanks for everything to God the
Father in the name of our Lord Jesus Christ*
(5:20).
How many of us give thanks in *everything*?

With this help from Paul, the great psychologist, we
should be able to *analyze the behavior patterns* of
people who come to us in their need. After writing
them down, we must prayerfully, with Scriptural
support, *plan the future corrections*. We must offer
hope and inspire the individual to desire change. We
must show him that those who know the Lord are given
grace and strength from the Lord to correct the *past*
and succeed in the *future*.

The people that know their God shall be
strong (Daniel 11:32).

Thou hast girded me with strength to battle
(2 Samuel 22:40).

I will strengthen thee (Isaiah 41:10).

They that wait upon the Lord shall renew
their strength; they shall mount up with
wings as eagles; they shall run and not be
weary, and they shall walk and not faint
(Isaiah 40:31).

When the needs are listed, the corrections established, and hope proclaimed, we are then able to list positive goals. Every depressed person needs something to look forward to. Where do you want to go? What do you want to learn? Where do you want to be a year from now? Do you want new friends? Do you want to help others? Do you want a better relationship with your husband? Do you need to plan time alone with each child?

Have the person write down his thoughts and take the paper with him. Set a future date to meet and review his progress. Before considering your job complete, check the physical condition of the person. Is he exhausted all the time? Does he consume a lot of sugar? We're not doctors, but I have spotted many health and diet problems in people and directed them to a physician.

I met Avis in Indianapolis, where with me she prayed to receive Christ. She had been depressed, so I sent her my tape on "Defeating Depression." She later sent me this letter:

For as long as I can remember I have had
two personalities—a laughing, friendly, kind

Avis and a sad, quiet, worried, mean Avis.
After marriage and during my childbearing
years, I was like Dr. Jekyll and Mr. Hyde. I
would often experience a meanness, a martyred attitude, and a desire to escape into my
shell. Also a craving for sweets would occur
along with heaviness and puffiness. My
doctors did not have a remedy for me other
than tranquilizers or an occasional cocktail.

I am well aware that my body chemistry
must have gone through severe changes each
month and that my *diet and activity was of
great influence*. Several years ago I went on a
diet control program, lost 35 pounds, and
exercised daily. Life was very different during
that time. Now I do not experience the
imbalance that used to occur. There is no
depression. Of course, along with that is the
fact that I am in a daily walk with Christ and
my spiritual life is blossoming. I must agree
with you, Florence, that the only real answer
to depression is a spiritual answer. Through
my search for a spiritual answer, I was led to
the diet and exercise plan, which was a physical answer. It appears that members of the
same family often have the same ailments. My
brother would also have moody spells of
hatefulness and aloneness, and nothing would
bring him out of them. His wife merely
continued to love him and wait until he "came
back."

He ate a lot of candy and drank too much
booze. A few years ago he had an attack of
something that affected his eyes and left him
with a large blind spot in the middle of one

eye. He was advised to watch his diet, particularly sugars, and his physical and emotional health was better.

He recently had another attack with his eyes without any further damage. He admitted he hadn't been following his diet plan. He saw then the importance of diet, disposition, and body health, and how they all worked together.

When I was typing your 18 steps of depression, he read them and admitted he had gone to step 14.

Quite often I remember your words and examples from the tapes. The word *joy* has had the most profound effect on my daily life. I thank you for the opportunity you gave me to pore over all those beautiful truths and soak up their meaning. My husband has admitted to me that he can sense my new attitude of love toward him. I must admit that I have a new attitude of love toward many other people too.

> With Love and Joy,
> Avis

Whenever I counsel people, I always give them an assignment. I make sure they have it in writing and stress how important it is that they do it. I also make clear that I don't want to hear from them until they have completed it. The assignment may be as simple as cleaning a closet or cooking a decent meal. It may be to read the book of Philippians or memorize a psalm.

Giving an assignment causes the sincere person to get to work and keeps the insincere from returning.

Many people want some additional help. From your

own reading suggest some *books*. Give them a copy of this book. Look over the bibliography in the back. Have some references available for their future study. Depressed people with a victory should be encouraged to prepare themselves to help other people.

Yesterday Lois called me. She is raising her two grandchildren and has many reasons to be depressed. She told me how much my tapes had helped her. "The other night I was so down. In the past I didn't know what to do when my spirits sank, but now I take out your tapes and listen. I put on your 'Game of Life' and did my ironing. As you spoke my depression lifted, and when you prayed at the end I prayed with you. I tell everyone to listen to your tapes." And Lois does.

Have tapes available to lend to those who need a lift as Lois did.

Find out what counselors, pastors, doctors, and psychologists are available in your area and refer any seriously disturbed person to one of these. It is best to give them a choice so they don't hold you accountable if they do not have good results.

Know the various agencies that provide mental health services in your town. And keep the numbers of crisis centers handy.

Counseling is hard work. I get more exhausted from a day of person-to-person contact than I do from speaking; yet the reward—the evidence of a changed life— is beautiful.

Barbara is a tall, stately girl who stood out like a model in a group of ladies in Tucson. As she approached me I instantly wished I had her youth and looks. Her soft blonde hair fell over her shoulders and bounced like the locks in shampoo commercials. Barbara looked like the All-American Beauty Queen, but Barbara was depressed. She told me she was on step 17, suicidal tendencies, and had been thinking of various ways to kill herself. She said, "I'm depressed and I have no reason for it."

As we began to probe her past, she mentioned that she gets depressed each November. She has kept her calendars for years, and in November each day is labeled "rotten day, rotten day, rotten day." She stays depressed until summer, when cheerleading practice begins, and she stays happy through football season. But when cheering stops she is no longer cheerful.

What was Barbara looking for in life? Attention. She wanted to be the focal point for the football team, but when the season closed so did she. "Is it possible," I asked, "that you get depressed because you need some attention?"

"Oh, no," she said quickly, "I don't do it on purpose."

As I asked about her depressions, she became excited about telling how her friends hover over her when she gets depressed. "They swarm around me and say, 'Cheer up, Barbara.' 'Poor, dear Barbara.' 'We can't have any fun, Barbara, when you're unhappy.' "

Barbara's real problem: She was self-centered and needed constant attention. Finally she admitted that she enjoyed people worrying over her, protecting her, and preventing her from committing suicide. She confessed that she really didn't want to kill herself but just wanted to make an attempt to get attention.

I explained how this desperate bid for attention would never satisfy, and we looked over the alternatives and consequences. Barbara agreed to confess her selfish nature as a sin and ask God to give her peace even if no one looked at her.

Barbara had to put aside her established behavior

patterns. She willingly changed when she understood the cause of her depression.

Some time later Barbara wrote me this letter and enclosed a picture of her sitting in a field of yellow flowers—in case I had forgotten what she looked like!

Dear Florence,

I wanted to thank you for talking with me at the Tucson seminar in April. You were just fantastic, and it made a total change in my attitudes and thoughts. Your talks were great, but what impressed me the most was that you cared enough to talk with me "special" and really put your words into action. Just talking with you encouraged me so much!

I feel I am over my depression and am very happy. I didn't want to write and thank you too soon. I had to make sure this was "real," and I am positive it is.

People asked me about your seminar and I didn't say much, but wanted them to see if they could notice a change in me. Within a week everyone commented on how I seemed different, and even now people are amazed at the change—must be real!

I work with a group called Young Life, and God has put this special high school gal in my life. She is a mirror image of me, and is going through depression, self-pity, etc.—all the things I went through. It's just beautiful to share with her, give her ideas on change from my experiences, and best of all to see her come out of depression! (Your tape really helped!) It's great to help others—makes me forget about me me me!

Again, thank you so very much. You are doing a great work for Christ and your reward will be great! God bless!

Thank you for teaching me what I wanted to know!

Love,

Barbara

12

What About
Teen Suicide?

In 1978, when I wrote the first edition of this book, there was little talk of teenage suicide. There were many cases, I'm sure, but we seldom heard about them because the majority were covered up by humiliated families who didn't want anyone to know what had happened. With a 300 percent increase in 20 years and with a rash of reported "cluster suicides" in affluent communities, teen suicide has suddenly become a major mental health concern.

USA Today dedicated their entire *Opinion* page to teen suicide on March 29, 1985. *America's Health*[1] did a cover story titled "Teen Suicide: What You Can Do About It." *Diagnosis*, a magazine for the medical profession, featured a lead article in November 1984 titled "Suicide-prone Patients: Warning Clues." Dr. James Dobson's *Focus on the Family* made available a "Fact Sheet on Teenage Suicide." Melodyland started a Suicide Hot Line and a report on teenage suicide. The National Committee for Youth Suicide Prevention was formed. CBS produced "Silence of the Heart,'' a story of a teenager's suicide and the shattered family he left behind.

Suddenly we have a problem on our hands. How did it happen? Teenage depression did not occur overnight. The causes behind these frightening facts didn't come out of the blue. They have been quietly breeding for many years.

Let's look behind the momentary problem to where it all began.

NEEDS OF CHILDREN

Psychologists have told us for years that the two basic needs we have in growing up are love and security. The Bible tells us, ''The greatest of these is love'' (1 Corinthians 13:13) and ''Love covers over a multitude of sins'' (1 Peter 4:8 NIV).

We learn as Christians that both love and security come from the Lord. ''The beloved of the Lord rest secure in him'' (Deuteronomy 33:12 NIV). ''He who fears the Lord has a secure fortress'' (Proverbs 14:26 NIV).

Children, however, derive their feelings of love and sense of security from their parents and their home situation. God's intention is for children to be born into loving, nurturing homes where there is a strong sense of security. The mother is to create the warmth while the father provides the security.

During the last 15 to 20 years as this generation of young people has been growing up, much of what the Bible considers normal has changed. As we have all been ''liberated,'' as mothers have gone to work, as children have been placed in day-care centers, as latchkey kids have come home to play in empty houses, as TV dinners have replaced family meals, as we've become a mobile society with uprooted roots, as television's version of family life has replaced our own—we have lost the vision of what God intended the family to be.

In spite of how well we may feel we've adjusted and how much better material environment we have for our children than what we grew up with, the hearts of our youth still yearn for the same things we did. We wanted to know that someone loved us and to know that if we had troubles in school there was a secure place to come home to.

We can change our lifestyles but we can't change the inbred needs of human nature.

How does a child perceive love? By touch and time. A child needs physical attention from someone who loves him. Isn't it amazing how a little baby knows when his mother is holding him rather than someone else who picks him up? A child craves a loving touch, and many teens today are screaming out for someone to love them.

Children equate love with touch and also with how much time we spend listening one-on-one to what they have to say.

I counseled one couple with marriage problems. They were both Christians caught up in the fast pace of the good life. They were separated, and each had an exciting job, huge mortgage payments, and expensive cars. They were working frantically to maintain their lifestyle. I pointed out that they hardly had a life, let alone a lifestyle. Somewhere in their explanation of their problems they mentioned little Jimmy. "Who is Jimmy?" I asked.

"Oh, he's our three-year-old son."

"Who takes care of him?"

"We divide the responsibility," the mother said. "He spends four days with his father and three with me.

Our separation doesn't bother him at all."

As I questioned them on the specifics of this arrangement, I found that when he was "with his father" he was at a day-care center and when he was "with his mother" he was at a babysitter. Since both worked into the evening or had social activities and the child was asleep when he was picked up, the only *actual* time they spent together was the drive to the sitter in the morning! They didn't have any idea how well the child was adjusting to their separation—they were too busy maintaining their lifestyle.

"Do you realize you are raising a depressed teenager?" I asked.

"But he's only three!" the mother stated defensively.

"I know, but the seeds of teen depression start with a child who doesn't feel loved, who doesn't spend time with his parents—preferably together—and who consequently feels rejected."

This was the first statement I had offered that seemed to make an impression on this well-meaning couple wrapped up in their own quest for love and security. They promised to spend the evening discussing whether the life of the child was worth a change in their own lifestyle.

NO ONE CARES

The one common thread in depressed teens is a feeling that no one cares.

"No one really loves me."

"If I died no one would even notice."

"It would be easier for everyone if I just weren't here."

"What's the use of living?"

If a young person feels that even one parent, but

preferably both, really accepts him as he is, approves of him as a real person, and gives him eye-to-eye attention at least occasionally, he will not want to end it all.

If he feels support from the family for his various activities and adventures and knows that home is a place of refuge where loving people await him, he will probably return.

Robert Frost said, "Home is the place where, when you have to go there, they have to take you in."[2]

But give him the opposite—an empty house, even equipped with large-screen TV, plenty of pizzas, and his own waterbed—and he'll feel lonely and rejected. An elaborate living room with no family sitting in it is nothing but a store window. There are so many lonely teenagers today who think that no one cares.

Sometimes we hear of a young man who has killed himself and left a note saying he did it because his girlfriend jilted him. We adults, with some perspective on life, can't imagine why such a little thing could trigger a suicide because when we were young we went through many broken-heart experiences and can remember grieving dramatically for a few days and then moving on again. What we don't realize is the pervasive loneliness that grips young people today who are convinced that their parents don't care.

One young man told me, "My mother keeps telling me, 'I can hardly wait for you to grow up and leave so I can make your room into a study.' "

A girl quoted her mother, "You're the last of the line, and I'm sick of raising children." I'm sure each mother was a well-meaning woman who had done her best, but the teens took the comments as rejections.

When they perceive that their parents have little time for them, are too busy with their own careers, or verbally wish they would grow up and get out, they seek their family relationships with similar teens. They seek love and security from friends, and, as a popular song says, "They're looking for love in all the wrong places."

Since many young teens establish sexual relationships with their friends, they have a bond with each other that is beyond our comprehension.

As they get the needed time and touch from their friends that we used to get from our family and are then rejected by that special person whose support they lived for, they may go into a depression that is far out of proportion to the actual facts.

GOD IS DEAD

The poet Coleridge said:

This soul hath been
Alone on a wide, wide sea:
So lonely 'twas that God himself
Scarce seem'd there to be.

To many teens, even Christian young people, God "scarce seems there to be." It was on the cover of *Time*, April 8, 1966, that a tombstone appeared proclaiming "God is Dead." From that time on, much of American society accepted the death of God as a liberating thought. Some have even tried to remove "In God We Trust" from our currency. Humanism—"Do your own thing," "If it feels good do it"—has become our new religion, culminating in the *me* generation of self-seekers.

When the family is being destroyed and God has been dismissed as dead, what does a young person have to hang on to? Is there any hope for this generation?

I was encouraged when on November 17, 1985, I bought a *Seattle Times* and was happily stunned to see on the cover of the enclosed *Pacific* magazine in large red letters "God Comes Back." I hoped this headline was a positive sign. The article, written about the same man who "tried to kill God" in 1966, William Hamilton, tells that he was a professor of theology at the Colgate Rochester Divinity School, "a nominal Baptist helping the seminary crank out other nominal Baptists."[3]

Mr. Hamilton still feels, "One of the greatest problems today is that men believe in God and that when they do so, they become dangerous."[4] Although he's done his best to "bring Jesus down from his perch in heaven, declare him a non-God and use him as a model for moral living,"[5] the article points out, "God has made a comeback, a big comeback, and he and his new conservative minions have trampled the likes of William Hamilton."[6]

We can take God's comeback as at least a sign that there is some hope.

HOPE FOR THIS GENERATION

The first step in any cure is facing the problem and wanting to do something about it. The widespread publicity about teen suicide has made us stop and listen. The epidemic has grabbed us by the throats and won't let us go until we promise to do something about it.

USA Today writes, "Just as there is no one cause for suicide, there is no one solution. But there are many ways to help our troubled young. Parents can help by being open and available. Friends can help by showing that they care. Teachers can help by seeking out troubled teens for talks. Everyone can help by recognizing suicide's warning signs."[7]

What are the causes and the warning signs? The following chart will give you some guidelines and ideas to discuss with a troubled teen to open up communication on possible background causes of present depression. Let him comment in any way and don't tell him his feelings are wrong, even if you know they are.

I took my son out for dinner one night and went over this list. I asked him to add any other symptoms he knew of from his friends. He contributed "poor eating habits," expressing how few of his friends had family meals and how many lived on junk food. He also mentioned how parents "knock their kids" and make them feel worthless. When I asked him about faith in God, he said, "Most kids, even Christians, don't really believe that God knows who they are, and they see no light at the end of the tunnel."

It is amazing how young people will really talk when you sit down away from the turmoil of the world, buy them a prime rib dinner, and let them know you intend to listen.

Charlotte Ross, Chairperson of the National Committee for Youth Suicide Prevention, said on TV one night, "We don't ask our children how they are doing because we're afraid they'll tell us."

Possible Causes of Teen Depression for Discussion:

Early rejection	Poor communications
Adoption	Poor eating habits
Family tension	Lack of love
Stepparents	Promiscuity
Frequent moves	Pregnancy

Loneliness
Learning disabilities
Overweight
Low self-worth
Sibling rivalry
Being jilted
High standards
Religious legalism

Abortion
Hard-rock music
Satanism
Drugs and alcohol
Fear of nuclear war
Suicide of friends
Lack of faith
Misconception of
   death

SYMPTOMS OF TEEN DEPRESSION

What are some warning signs that show us a teen is in trouble? While the symptoms in Chapter 3 are relevant to all ages, there are a few additional ones that seem to specifically show up in teens.

Behavior changes. Any change in attitude—sudden burst of temper, lashing out at family members, withdrawal from usual activities—should be examined as possible depression.

Lowering of grades. Any sudden drop in grades or interest in school may signify depression and/or a use of drugs.

Different friends. When old friends are dropped and new ones either appear to be of a questionable nature or don't appear at all, you should be suspicious of drugs and depression.

Dazed look and bored attitude. These are again symptoms of both depression and some kind of drug use. Since 50 percent of teen suicides are known to be drug-related, these two problems often go hand-in-hand.

Noticeable changes in eating habits. Any eating disorder is a sign of depression: anorexia (starving to get thin enough to satisfy a shaky self-image) or bulimia (gorging on food and then self-inducing vomiting). One girl told me she had been doing this after every meal for two years and her parents had never appeared to notice.

Changes in sleep patterns. Use of drugs can cause constant sleepiness or a hyperactive personality. Even without drugs a severely depressed child will often have trouble sleeping or will seem to be passing out at any possible opportunity. As with adults, the sleep pattern may swing in either direction, but a change means trouble.

Talk of suicide. Before a youngster takes his own life he usually runs the idea by the family to pick up their reaction. If the father says, "Only an idiot would kill himself" and the mother asks, "Why would a good boy like you from a fine family like ours even mention such a thing?" the teen will know that he and his parents are on different planets. If your child brings the subject up, listen and feel out his opinion; ask why teens are doing this. Don't moralize or preach. Remember, he's asking you if you really love him.

Written signals. Frequently the troubled teen will write notes that give clues to his feelings. His school papers may allude to death and he may write practice suicide notes and wait for your reaction. Remember, he doesn't think you care.

Giving away possessions. If a teen starts doling out his radio or his favorite sweater, or making lists of what he wants his friends to have when he's gone, be sure to take this unusual pattern seriously.

Attempted suicide. Once a teen has tried and failed, there is a high probability that he or she will try again. Many parents look at this attempt as an attention-getter, but it should be considered as valid. Check the house for weapons and drugs. When a teen returns from the hospital after an attempted suicide, be aware that this is the time he is most apt to try it again.

WHAT CAN PARENTS DO?

What steps can we take to reduce the chances that some young person we know might take his own life? Just by reading this chapter you have already seen that there is a problem.

Listen to what you say to your children. Do you call them dummies? Do you say they're the slow one? The clumsy one? The stubborn one? Whatever you say stays in their minds. One girl I talked with, an adopted child of Christian leaders, told me that each time her mother got mad at her she would call her "illegitimate" and say "you'll probably turn out like your mother." I assume she thought—if she thought at all—that the child wouldn't know what she meant, but as she grew up she understood, and she fulfilled this negative prophecy by getting pregnant as a teenager.

What our children hear us say does influence their opinion of themselves. A low self-image leads to depression.

Keep Christianity as a vibrant, positive influence in the home and not as a list of all the things Christians can't do. So many legalistic homes where the parents live in church half the time produce quietly rebellious children who suddenly run away, take drugs, or get pregnant. If Jesus isn't exciting in your life, His rules aren't going to make much sense to your children.

Listen to what they have to say. I've had so many teens in trouble say to me, "I tried to tell her but she wouldn't listen." My son seems to want to talk most at about midnight, so I brighten up and listen. I realize I can sleep when he's gone from home but I can never make up for what he wanted to tell me but couldn't.

Study up on drugs and know the symptoms of each type so you would recognize them if they were sitting in front of you. So few Christian adults have any idea of what's freely available to teens today. I heard on a Dallas TV newscast that a new manufactured drug had hit the streets and was selling for a few dollars a fix. "It's cheap because it hasn't been out long enough to be banned," the announcer stated. "Once the government makes it illegal, the price will go up."

Let them know that life has problems, and teach them how to deal with disappointments rather than run away from them.

Timothy Allen, former assistant principal of El Toro High School in California, says:

> I think alcoholism is the biggest problem. One out of sixteen seniors is harmfully involved in drinking on a daily basis. . . . The kid breaks up with his girl, can't get along with his folks. The chemical is the only thing he can trust. It works every time. These kids aren't taught to deal with failure in a normal way. Rather than deal with it, they medicate it.[8]

How many of us as parents medicate the pains of life rather than deal with them? Allen adds, "Parents today are afraid to be parents. They have lost control of their homes."[9]

A 17-year-old boy at a teenage alcohol program who had been a polybuser (both alcohol and drugs) explained, "You get addicted to the whole escape. No problems, no worries; it's the twilight zone. I didn't want to be left out. I wanted to be part of the in group."

His great escape led him into selling drugs and later stealing. Ultimately the drug treatment cost about 10,000 dollars a month.[10] Yes, a month!

Discuss the fear of nuclear war. When Fred was in high school he came home and said, "We were talking about suicide today." I gulped and listened. "There's going to be a war, we're all going to be drafted, we'll be killed by a nuke, so we might as well get it over with now." Fifty-seven percent of our young people expect to get killed by nuclear war before they reach adulthood.[11] Your child may well have this fear but never told you.

Make sure they understand clearly how pregnancy happens. We think that with all the loose talk today and sex education in the schools they must know everything. Yet they are amazingly unaware that it could happen to them. In San Diego there has been what was labeled a "rash of teenage pregnancies." The community was amazed that these kids didn't know better, and one columnist tried to put a note of cheer on the epidemic when he wrote, "Fortunately, most of the pregnancies end in abortion." Unfortunately, many also end in suicide.

Know where your child is and don't give him unsupervised afternoons at your home or anyone else's. In the past teens necked in parked cars. Now they get pregnant in mother's bed at 3:00 in the afternoon. I know we can't watch them every minute, but we must be aware of what goes on and not make it easy for them.

Don't let your child join a Dungeons and Dragons club even though it may be on the school grounds. This involvement leads to perverse behavior, and many suicides have been linked to what started out as a game.

Most important of all, let your child know that you love him.

Pat Nordman wrote to me about her son. She began, "I am now reading your book *Blow Away the Black Clouds*. I would like to share with you the story of my oldest son's suicide. Your book has been a great blessing."

Charles was quiet, brilliant, and a perfectionist, but he was uncommunicative and unable to express his feelings. He was on drugs for several years, yet his parents didn't know it. In his third year in college he came home for Thanksgiving and confessed that he had fears, confusion, depression, and suicidal thoughts.

"He was extremely nervous; he couldn't stand noise; he wanted to be alone. He was physically sick several times and he kept saying, 'I've got to get my head together.' He wanted to sleep all the time, and later we found an empty bottle of sleeping pills in his room."

When he went back to school he tried to commit suicide, but the authorities never called his parents. At Christmas vacation he returned home, went to the woods behind his house, and shot himself to death.

Pat writes, "Tragedy is very special and it is very fragile. It also carries a great responsibility. Chuck's death hurts so deeply, but through our tears we hope to see other lives saved. Chuck's untimely, unnatural death cannot and will not be in vain." Pat is now available to speak to groups and is often on the radio in hopes that her testimony will be used to prevent other suicides.

Some of her comments are:

"We expected too much from him. . . . We didn't give him a chance to be young."

"We didn't let him be himself. We wanted a carbon copy of our own work habits and ideals."

"We didn't take time to tell him we loved him; we didn't physically hold him."

Pat's advice: "Love your child even before he's born. Forget a spic-and-span house for the first five years. Rock the child, and read and sing to him. Don't send him but go with him to church and picnics. Most important, *touch* him: Put your arm around him and rub his back."

What can grandparents do? Follow any of the previous suggestions, but most of all remember that you have a very special spot in the heart of each grandchild. You can be a positive loving, hugging influence that the child may not get at home. Never make negative comparisons; just give that extra love and stability the child needs. Let him talk to you without a sense of condemnation so that when there's a burden on his heart he'll know you'll listen. Develop a trusting relationship and then don't betray the trust by quoting in public some cute saying he made in private. Remember that one loving grandparent can cover a multitude of sins.

What should the church do? How great it would be if the church worked to *prevent* problems instead of reacting in shock when they happen! I am so excited today as I travel to many different churches to see how many are aware of people's problems and how many are doing something about them. The church needs to teach its youth about the danger of premarital sex, drugs, and depression leading to possible suicide. Discussion should be open and direct and not preachy. My chapter for teens in *Out of the Cabbage Patch* explains and refutes the six reasons teens give for why it's all right to "sleep around," and this would be a good place for the church youth group to start. Each time I have given this to young people there has been a deathly hush and riveted attention.

One girl came up to me after I spoke at a large Christian high school and said, "Wow, I didn't know any adult really knew how we felt!"

We must do our homework in the church by training our youth leaders on how to spot and deal with these problems. We must have the names and numbers on hand of the local hot lines and crisis counselors. We must study up on drugs and be alert to the signs of those who may be on them. We must make the family a top priority in our churches and teach them to communicate with each other.

One Christian leader told me that her son was in a rehabilitation center to cure his drug addiction. In order to keep him there in the program, the parents had to come two evenings a week, sit across the table from the boy, and, with a counselor's prodding, talk together for three hours in a row. She said this was the most difficult thing she had ever done. At first no one had anything to say. After a while they began to vent their anger on the boy and the counselor had to intervene. Eventually they learned how to communicate in a positive and pleasant manner.

Wouldn't it be a novel idea for churches to bring families together, make them sit looking at each other, with one outsider as a monitor, and teach them how to find some common ground of interest upon which they could build some meaningful relationships? Why wait until the child is on drugs before finding out what's been boiling inside him for years? Why wait until the husband is ready to walk out before resolving the conflicts?

The reason the Mormon Church is growing so fast despite all its problems is because of its emphasis on the family and its clear instructions on how to conduct a family night. Few people choose a church for its doctrine; they go to the church that meets their needs.

The church should help parents to set consistent guidelines of standard behavior for their teens so that they are all speaking with one voice. In Pasadena, Texas, the community has formed a Concerned Citizens Council. Spurred by the rash of teen suicides in their area, they got together and came up with acceptable modes of conduct for their youth. They also printed up a page on "Guidelines for talking with your child about drug use."

Why can't our churches tackle these problems and help the distraught parents rather than look the other way and hope it will go away?

Dr. Keith Schuchard, in a speech titled "The Family Versus the Drug Culture" (presented in May 1978 in Atlanta), suggested:

> The main thing that parents are up against is unhealthy peer pressure, which is reinforced or often even created by a highly commercialized, attractively packaged, seductively advertised youthful drug and rock culture. But peer pressure can be reversed and redirected into more healthy channels by cooperating groups of parents, by parental peer pressure. When a youngster says, "But everybody is doing it," he usually means his friends. If three friends are no longer doing it because their parents have banded together and said, "You are not doing it and here is why," then within that 13-year-old's mind "Everybody is not doing it." If thirty parents band together and say, "You are not doing it and here is why," then the peer pressure within a class or a neighborhood can be reversed. Better, if 300 parents

say you are not, then a child grows up in an entirely different community. After all, SOCIETY, with capital letters, is you and me; we make it up by two's and three's and dozens.

Parents will have a lot more fun and a lot closer sense of community if they carry this out in the company of other parents. In a time of powerful adolescent peer pressures, parents need peer pressure too.

The Spirit of Freedom Ministries in New Orleans has published some parental guidelines in a booklet titled *The Drug Crisis—a word to Mom and Dad.*

1. Provide the teenager with as much love, understanding, and approval as possible.
2. Maintain good communications between you and your child. Remember, this is a two-way street.
3. Create an awareness of the parental and family influence in developing *values* and *standards*.
4. Set a good example for your child.
5. If necessary, seek professional help *early*.[12]

Let's help our families prevent problems by constructive action within the church.

Besides dealing with the human problems that teens face, we must also let them know that there is a God who cares for them and that they can know Him in a personal way through accepting the Lord Jesus into their hearts. They must be taught at least John 3:16 in a way that makes it real in their lives, so they know that God loves them enough to have sent His Son to die for them that they might have everlasting life. So many young people I talk to in churches have no concept of eternal life. Some think death is a perpetual drug high.

One counselor friend of mine was working with a Christian family whose teen daughter took a mixed overdose of drugs to commit suicide. It took her 27 agonizing days of convulsions to die. The counselor went up to the floor in the hospital where the teens on drug cures were housed and brought a group of them down to see this girl as she screamed in pain, writhing on the bed, throwing herself around, having convulsions. The "druggies" watched in horror at this pitiful scene, and one spoke for the group as she said, "I had no idea this was how you died. I thought you just took the pills and that was the end of it."

The church needs to teach teens about death, about heaven and hell—not in an emotional, threatening way but in straightforward, no-nonsense terms so they won't be caught saying, "I had no idea this was how you died."

A potential suicide victim wrote to Ann Landers:

> I have a few words of advice for those who suspect someone they know is contemplating suicide. Don't ignore the signs. Confront them and let them know you want to help. A few simple words, such as, "You are a valuable person," or, "I care about you," will do wonders. Make him understand that everyone is unique even though he might not think so. Tell him today. Tomorrow may be too late.[13]

13

When It's
Too Late

When the call comes that your friend's son has shot himself on the back patio or your neighbor's 15-year-old girl has taken an overdose of drugs and is dying in the hospital, what do you do? The majority of us wish we hadn't answered the phone. We just don't know what to say or what to do.

Jan, a woman who attended CLASS and whose brother committed suicide, later wrote to me:

> Our Christian culture needs to be sensitive to the needs of those who have lost a loved one to suicide, and to assist and encourage those who have friends or family that may have tried and failed in taking their own life.
>
> Understanding the emotions of "suicide survivors" is of great importance. Knowing the processes of shock, relief, catharsis, depression, guilt, and anger is necessary in ministering to these hurting people. It is believed that these grieving emotions are felt ten times

greater than a normal loss through death. In the case of our family it was nearly ten years before we could openly discuss the emotions we all went through. Oh, we talked or mentioned my brother, but not his death. I now know through interaction with others who have suffered a similar loss that this is normal. One of the lines I use when teaching my workshop on suicide is "Suicide is a singular act with plural effect."[1]

Go immediately. If there ever was a time when your friend or relative needed you, it's now. Don't worry about what you will say: You are not on Candid Camera, and you do not have to perform, but you must go and be available for whatever needs arise. Since the parents are loaded with guilt, your not coming to their side would verify in their minds that they are to blame.

A suicide survivor wrote to Ann Landers:

One of the most difficult things we must deal with is the number of close friends, neighbors, and business associates who refuse to acknowledge our loss or offer sympathy.

Please advise the world that when suicide strikes, the grief is as painful as after any other type of death. The survivors need sympathy and kind words, perhaps even more than when a loved one dies from an illness.[2]

Listen and protect. Remember that your ears are more important than your mouth. You aren't expected to produce words of wisdom but to listen. Let the mother cry; let the father slam doors. Don't tell them they shouldn't be doing this. Whatever helps them vent their anger or release their guilt should not be condemned. Unless you've been through this type of death yourself, you don't really know what you would do. One mother went out and pruned her roses. While this relaxed the terrible tension for her, friends came over and told her she shouldn't be pruning "at a time like this." It wasn't "right."

As you listen to the griever, also be aware of what other people might do or say that would hurt, and try to protect your friend. Family arguments can easily ensue over whose fault this suicide was. If possible, stave these off with "Neither one of you was to blame. It's not your fault."

Remove guilt. One of the first emotions the parents have along with shock is *guilt*, and they innately try to place the blame somewhere. It's a huge burden on their backs, and the faster they can take it off and give it to someone else the better they think they'll feel. No matter where they place it verbally, the guilt stays with them. Ultimately the awareness that the child made the decision, that he's the one who pulled the trigger, will ease the overwhelming feeling of personal responsibility.

Dr. David Baldwin writes that one of the best things the family doctor, pastor, or friend can do is to try to lift this burden of guilt that comes with the suicide of a child.

> Once parents attain this conviction, and realize that—whether as the result of inner turmoil, a temporary chemical imbalance, whatever—the suicide was the child's act and not theirs, they'll at least have assuaged their guilt.[3]

Don't tell them why it happened. Somehow we

comforters seem led to tidy up the mess of suicide by explaining it away. We say stupid things.

> "I saw this coming a long while ago."
> "If only you'd kept him in Christian schools."
> "You should never have let him go to those school dances."
> "Everyone knew he was on drugs."
> "If you hadn't gone to work, this wouldn't have happened."
> "If only you'd made him go to youth group."

And on and on.

Remember, you don't have to say much. It's your presence that counts. My father taught me a little saying that I'm sure he must have felt I needed: "Better to keep your mouth shut and be thought a fool than to open it and remove all doubt."

Don't judge. It's so easy to open our mouths and say things we regret later, to heap judgment on already-grieving parents. Don't judge their ability as parents or their spirituality. Don't decide whether or not this suicide victim is going to heaven. The parents are already in doubt, but the only positive hope they may be clinging to at the moment is that they will see this child in heaven. Don't pull this shaky rug out from under them. If the child had a conversation with you about his salvation or faith in Christ, this story would be an encouragement for you to share.

Help them plan a normal funeral. Because of the social stigma connected with suicide, parents can often be persuaded to bypass the normal grieving procedures and pretend the whole thing never happened. In months to pass this omission becomes a negative emotion, and the parents going through the stages of grief regret that they did not "do it properly."

Sometimes well-meaning friends keep the mother from seeing the body. Horrible as it may be, in most cases if she wishes to see the dead child, she should not be held back. Obviously, if she can't bear to see him, don't force her.

Dr. Baldwin tells of a nephew who shot himself in the head with his father's gun. Naturally, the father was loaded with guilt since it was his gun. The mother wondered if she had belittled the boy too much.

Dr. Baldwin writes:

> Then there was the pain, indescribably intense, worse than they'd even known. Their anger, grief, and shame were reflected in the way they handled Joey's funeral arrangements. Wanting to get the whole thing over with as quickly as possible, they decided to have neither viewing nor visiting hours, and no reception at their house after the funeral. Nor did they accept phone calls.
>
> If I'd had the experience I've since acquired with the after-effects of a teen-age suicide, I'd have urged a different course. For example, a teen-age suicide's funeral should be conducted as it would be for any other teen-ager. Indeed, funeral proceedings are an important part of helping a family regain emotional balance.[4]

So if you are a part of the victim's family, encourage them to do what they would have done if he had died of more accepted causes. Help them choose a casket, plan visiting hours, go through whatever rituals are normal for their church, and have a funeral where positive comments are made about the victim.

Check in with them later. Don't go home from the funeral, say "I'm glad that's over," and disappear from view, as so many people do. Check in, call up, and drop over. Once the shock stage is over a deep guilt sets in, and the survivors feel that everyone has deserted them. This perceived abandonment adds to their feelings of self-condemnation and triggers marriage problems, suicidal thoughts for themselves, and questioning whether or not they are going crazy.

They often sit in gloom reviewing comments people have made and deciding they were all condemnations. Siblings of the victim may feel somehow responsible for the death and sometimes contemplate suicide themselves. They feel neglected and left out as all the attention has been placed on the parents and the memory of the victim. My daughter Lauren's book *What You Can Say When You Don't Know What To Say* has a chapter titled "The Forgotten Griever," which was inspired by how she felt when my sons died and we did not recognize her needs in our own grief experience.

Remember that when the eulogies are over, the casket is closed, and the geraniums have dropped their blossoms, the survivors are facing the stark reality that Junior is gone. His room is empty, his place at the table is unfilled, and a pall of shame hangs heavily over the house. Other people have gone back to work and they seem to chatter about such trivia. People at church don't mention Junior any more. It's almost as if he never lived. But he's still alive in the heart of that grieving mother and in the soul of the struggling father.

Go over and let them tell you how they feel. You can be the arms of the Lord around a family in need.

14

When All Else
Fails

Let's assume that you have done everything I've suggested plus a list of creative cures of your own but are still depressed. You have had a poor self-image as far back as you can remember and have never been really happy for any length of time. You've got a story to tell if anyone cared to listen, but they tune you out. You get angry easily but try to keep it under control since the pastor's sermon made it clear that anger is a sin. You know you should be smelling roses along the pathway of life, but the bushes come up all thorns for you.

Since you started reading this book, you've tried everything I suggested. You've taken an Image Improvement Course with Joanne Wallace, lost 40 pounds with Neva Coyle, and exercised with Stormie Omartian. You've cleaned drawers and organized your household with Emilie Barnes and have gone so far as to alphabetize all the books in the pastor's study. You've analyzed your stress, read books on positive thinking, attended three Bible studies a week, and confessed your faults to everyone who would listen. You've been given verses by the church counselor and prayed piously with the pastor, but you're still miserable.

What do you do when all else fails? If you have done all you know to do and have sought the Lord's will in your life and have still come up empty, perhaps there are some hidden problems in your past that you have not wanted to look at or some events in your childhood that were so traumatic that you blanked them out totally from your conscious memory. Much as we would like to feel that there is no incest in our church or that the troubles of childhood are best forgotten or that time heals all wounds or that forgiveness will erase the pains of the past, there are still many women in our church bodies who are carrying heavy burdens of hurts, victimizations, rejections, guilt, and shame and who have tried unsuccessfully to give it all to Jesus.

Patsy Clairmont demonstrated this situation clearly at our CLASS in Champaign, Illinois. The stage was decorated in an autumn arrangement of gourds and pumpkins. Patsy picked up one of the pumpkins and said, "This represents the pains of my past. I carried them around but I didn't know where to put them." She then tried stuffing the round pumpkin into her pocket and her handbag, but it wouldn't fit. She put it behind her back so others wouldn't see it, but she couldn't hide it. Even if she were to swallow it, the lump would stick out somewhere. In Patsy's case when she pushed the pains of her past way down inside her, she went into depression, followed by anxiety attacks which led to agoraphobia. You can't just hide these problems and hope they'll go away; you have to deal with them, work through them, and resolve your feelings.

CHRISTIAN BAND-AIDS

Much of what passes for Christian counseling today is putting a large Band-Aid of wishful thinking over a festering wound and then wondering why it doesn't heal. In the past few years I have listened to women with problems that have passed all my imaginations and whom I could not in any sense of good conscience send home to clean a drawer or memorize a verse.

One lady was molested at four years old by her brother. She was constantly watched by the man next door, who raped her at 12. Her uncle kept feeling her whenever he could get her alone. She got pregnant at 15 and had to get married knowing in her heart that her husband couldn't possibly ever love her. Her younger brother was molested by a homosexual neighbor and became gay, later enticing her own son and leading him in the same direction. Her husband's business failed, they lost their home, and when she found that her 15-year-old daughter was pregnant, she wanted to run away and leave it all behind. This lady had armloads of pumpkins and she didn't know where to put any of them. She had tried to hide them, but there were too many to conceal.

You might say, "Isn't this some isolated case you dug up to make a point?" "Where did you find this loser?" "Surely she doesn't go to our church."

I wish this were an isolated case, but she is representative of so many women in fine churches who have kept their problems to themselves. Some have been afraid to tell anyone, and some have dared to with disastrous results. The last thing a victim wants to hear from some pious pretender is, "If you were really a good Christian and read your Bible, you'd be all right."

Emotions Anonymous was formed for those whose

emotional problems interfere with their lives and relationships and who may be suffering symptoms of panic, despair, depression, anxiety, remorse, or low self-esteem.

> Unwarranted guilt feelings often are responsible for great unhappiness and incidents of intense depression.... Suppressed anger with no release and subsequent guilt for feeling angry and resentful can be a circular downward spiral leading to serious emotional difficulty. A supportive atmosphere can free the sufferer from the bonds of silence.[1]

Where should we find supportive atmospheres that could break the bonds of silence? Shouldn't this be in the Christian community? Recently Lana Bateman, author of *God's Crippled Children*, spoke at a retreat. The women opened up and broke "the bonds of silence." As Lana helped them in healing the hurts of the past, the women went home with a new sense of freedom and relief. They shared with their husbands what had happened.

These religious men later got together and decided that these problems had been greatly exaggerated. "Our wives don't really have any serious problems, and if they do they shouldn't talk about them." They suggested that next year the speaker should be "some sweet lady who would do some harmless Bible studies"—in other words, someone who would put a big Band-Aid over the hurting hearts.

What those men don't know is how many of their wives called secretly begging for some help in dealing with their problems, not the least of which were their sanctimonious husbands.

Our CLASS staff was called to train the adult Sunday school teachers at a large church. I explained that few people come to church anymore because it's the thing to do or because of any burning passion for God's Word, but rather to find a spiritual answer for their emotional and physical needs. Recognizing this premise, we teachers and speakers had better find the needs and do our best to fill them. I suggested that each teacher pass out a paper to his or her class members and have them write down their personal problems without including their names so that the teachers would have an idea of what they were facing each Sunday.

Later one teacher wrote me:

I must tell you that when you said we had people with deep problems in our Sunday school classes, I thought to myself "maybe somewhere else, but not here." I felt I knew my people and didn't intend to follow your suggestion; however, the next Sunday I looked at them a little differently and sensed some hurting hearts. I looked into their eyes as you had mentioned and I saw three kinds, as you had said: those holding back pools of pain, those that seemed frightened, and the dead eyes. On the spur of the moment I handed them all some notebook paper and they began to write. I watched in awe as some filled both sides of their paper. That week as I read the messages they had written to me I realized I didn't know them at all and I had surely not been meeting their needs. I thought you'd be interested in my list. Out of sixteen women, six are divorced, and here are their other problems:

Mother of homosexual
Mother whose young adult son died
Lady in wheelchair who was stricken with
   sudden disease
Former wife of homosexual
Mother whose son fell through a ceiling to
   his death
Daughter whose mother committed suicide
Mother who lost her young children in a
   divorce
Lady involved in a cult that wouldn't let her
   go
Lady whose unemployed husband com-
   mitted suicide three months ago
Lady diagnosed with Alzheimer's disease
   three years ago
New stepmother
Lupus victim
Grandmother of brain-damaged child whose
   parents are divorced and away from the
   Lord
Lady whose husband died suddenly on vaca-
   tion
Wife of a heart transplant patient
Mother whose teenage son died of cancer

Now that I've seen the light, or is it the
darkness, my whole approach to Sunday
school teaching has changed. My stylish ladies
who appear to be smiling on Sunday are
hurting all week long and I'm determined to
meet their needs.

Much as we would like to ignore the rash of current
traumas and use "Pray about it" as the aspirin for every

pain, we must be willing to look behind the symptoms to the causes even if they don't fit our spiritual mold. We must provide a warm, loving, nonjudgmental atmosphere in our churches and Bible studies where hurting men and women will be free to break "the bonds of silence."

Les Stobbe, editor of Here's Life Publishers, writes:

> Based on frequent one-on-one interaction at writers conferences, I find that women in churches are afraid to share openly with their pastors because they have been too often told to go home and be submissive. Pastors need to start listening, believing what Christian women are telling them—not merely to men trying to cover up wife abuse, child abuse, even sexual abuse of children.

So often a lady will come to me and say, "I've never told this to anyone in my life before." Frequently she is a pastor's wife, Bible teacher, or Christian speaker. She's never dared to tell anyone because she was afraid they wouldn't like her anymore, they would blame her for the circumstances she fell into, or—worst fear of all—they would make light of it and tell her that as a Christian she should have forgiven and forgotten by now. Since all victims feel guilty, the last thing they want is someone who will put more guilt upon them. They are already covered with simplistic spiritual Band-Aids and they are juggling more pumpkins than they can handle.

CHRISTIAN TRUTH

The Bible tells us that God made us in His image and

slightly lower than the angels. In Psalm 139 David calls out to God and affirms, "You created my inmost being; you knit me together in my mother's womb. . . . I am fearfully and wonderfully made. . . . Your eyes saw my unformed body" (NIV).

God knew us before we were born and wanted us to be like Him, but He didn't say that life would be perfect, that if we believed in His Son we would be emotionally stable and totally healthy. He knew we would sin and He grieved over the problems the Hebrews got themselves into. David, a man after God's own heart, the one who taught the Ten Commandments to others, violated three of them: covetousness, adultery, and murder. God forgave David and allowed him to stay as king, yet David still suffered the death of his child, rebellion in his household, and incest and rape in his family.

If God created us and yet we find ourselves depressed and discouraged, what does He want us to do about our inner pain? He wants to guide us as we seek for the source of our problems.

> Search me, O God, and know my heart; test me and know my anxious thoughts. See if there is any offensive way in me, and lead me in the way everlasting (Psalm 139:23,24 NIV).

While some of us are able to change our behavior patterns with the help of a competent Christian counselor or pastor, those who still find themselves making the same mistakes and who after trying all known solutions are still defeated may need to search with God into their hearts, may need to be tested to know their inner thoughts. Some may need to go back through their childhood in their minds, take off some Band-Aids that have been covering up their hurts, and learn the truth. "Then you will know the truth, and the truth will set you free" (John 8:32 NIV).

CHRISTIAN HEALING

How do we know if we need some deeper examination of our past? Have we tried the basic steps in overcoming depression but still see that little black cloud hovering over our head? Do we often feel guilty but have no reason why? Are there gaps in the memory of our childhood? Some people remember no Christmases, some nothing from age six to ten. Are we stuck emotionally in our childhood? Some adults still talk as children or react as third-graders. Have we been hurt so much that we've shut off our emotions and no longer feel anything in life? David Seamands in his book *Healing of Memories* quotes one of his clients:

> I guess I learned to cope with all this by just never allowing myself to feel anything. I didn't dare let myself feel good in the occasional happy times because I knew they couldn't last. And I didn't dare allow myself to cry or feel down because I just had to keep going. I guess the truth of the matter is that I've been afraid to let myself feel. And now I don't know how.[2]

A girl handed me the following note during a coffee break in one of my seminars:

> Could you plesae say something on how to come to the point where *you do* deal with a past emotional trauma (any trauma) that

you've been suppressing. I've been trying to
cry for years. I want to deal with it so I can
go on. It is not one major crisis but many,
with one in particular I'm trying to deal with
now. What do I do with past scars?

This girl had put the brakes on her feelings because
they were too painful to face. Somewhere in the past
she had gone through something that hurt so badly that
she still can't even cry.

Seamands says that we do have the ability to block
out things we're not able to face, but—

though we may block out the pain quite
unintentionally, we still suffer the consequences. . . . It requires a great deal of
continuous emotional and spiritual energy to
keep the memory in its hidden place. . . .
Since these memories are not allowed to enter
through the door of our minds directly, they
come into our personalities (body, mind and
spirit) in disguised and destructive ways. These
denied problems go underwater and later reap-
pear as certain kinds of physical illnesses,
unhappy marital situations, and recurring
cycles of spiritual defeat.[3]

The incest victim is one who has little hope of
complete recovery without some type of Christian healing. He or she manifests many unexplained symptoms,
such as migraine headaches, asthma, body pain, frigid-
ity, chronic overweight, guilt, anger at his or her
children, and long-term depression. In my chapter on
incest in *Lives on the Mend* I tell the story of one victim,
Jan Frank, and her ten steps to recovery. Jan had many

symptoms and has been through several types of therapy, culminating with two days of counseling and prayer with Lana Bateman for Christian healing of the pains of the past.

If you fit some of the symptoms I've mentioned, what should you do about it? Since this is not an area to deal with lightly, you should first pray and see if God is leading you to work positively with this collection of complaints and to seek His healing power.

Lana first assigns an individual to read her book, *God's Crippled Children*, and to pray for God's leading, for if God is not in control no type of healing will work for long. When people call for counsel, Lana asks questions about the sincerity of the request. If it's to please their mother or just seems like a positive thing to do, she suggests that they pray about it some more. Lana says, "Unless the person sincerely wants to remove every obstacle that stands between them and God's perfect will for their life, the time of counsel and prayer will have only a limited effect."

What can you do by yourself? Read Seamands' *Healing of Memories* and Lana's *God's Crippled Children*. As you are going through these, write down in a notebook all the childhood memories that the Lord brings to your mind. Look over these lists prayerfully and ask the Lord to show you any consistent threads that run through your childhood. If you have some gaps or shadowy memories, check them out with some aunt or cousin who was around then. Be aware of the relative's immediate reaction more than their words, for if they were involved in or knowledgeable about some traumatic incident that happened to you, their response may be startled or defensive. The more vehemently they tell you nothing happened the more you will know something did. Don't argue or get defensive yourself, for remember that your purpose in looking back is not to stir up trouble but to find some new clues that will open up your mind as to why you are depressed today. Unexplained and illogical black clouds can often be swept away when we put together some of the pieces of the past.

In an article "Pains May Be Body Talking To Mind," Dr. Rick Ingrasci tells that "the medical Establishment is starting to take the mind-body interaction more seriously through research on the relationship between thoughts and emotions and the immune, glandular, and nervous systems."[4]

He suggests that the individual sit down and write out fill-in-the-blank sentences such as: "I feel an asthma attack coming on whenever _____. He has found patients more able to diagnose their own problems when they sit down and thoughtfully write out their own analysis.[5]

In my own assigning of women to journalize their feelings daily, I've seen amazing results. "Now I see why I react to my husband this way." "Now I understand why I keep buying shoes." It is amazing how many of our background problems can be self-discovered if we only take the time to sit down and write what comes to our minds.

Sometimes just asking yourself a few questions might trigger some explanations. A depressed pastor told me he didn't really have his heart in his work. I said, "When did you decide to go into the ministry?"

He replied, "I didn't decide; I was told by Mother from the time I was a child that I was to be a pastor. She often reminded me that there had been a pastor in every generation of her family and that I was the chosen one. She would smile and say, 'You wouldn't want to be the one to break the chain.' "

As he poured this out to me, he suddenly stopped and cried out, "That's why I'm not happy—I didn't have any say in it! I just didn't want to break the chain." In a matter of minutes he had discovered his own childhood problem that was crippling his current ministry. Once he made an adult evaluation of his life and blew away his previously unexplained black cloud, he decided he *did* want to be a pastor after all, with or without his mother's direction. He was then freed of his depression and was able to put his efforts wholeheartedly into the discipling of his people.

What can you do with the help of others? Even as I asked that one question of the pastor that opened his mind to the pains of the past, so a friend could do the same for you.

Perhaps you can find a friend whom you can trust, one who will help you through the maze of memories. Perhaps you could help each other. Lana never set out to have a ministry, but as her own pains of the past were healed, God sent people with problems to her door. Now her Philippian Ministries trains other people to life the burdens from the backs of the heavy-laden.

What kind of person could help you?

An accepting person. The first requirement is that a person has accepted the Lord Jesus into his or her life and is willing to accept you as you are without judging your life. We will never be totally honest with a person whom we fear will judge us; we need freedom in expression as we examine ourselves. An accepting person will listen and love and then put your past pains as far as the east is from the west.

Without the power of the Lord Jesus to convict us, these reviews would be little more than Trivial Pursuit. Both our prayer partner and ourselves must believe that

"I can do all things through Christ who strengthens me" (Philippians 4:13).

An affirming partner. You need a faithful friend who will allow you to cry without forcing you to cheer up, who will be a true partner, equally yoked with the same purpose in mind, and who will gently pick you up when you stumble on some rock of resentment. This partner should reaffirm your worth in the eyes of God.

An analytical personality. You'll want someone who thinks logically and can hold your life together in some sequence. This person should take notes of the hidden hostilities you expose as you review your memories and remember to bring you back to them in your time of prayer.

Hopefully you will find a friend who has a sensitive spirit and a gift of discernment, one who knows a guilt-producing grudge when it appears. He or she should question your attitudes on your mother, father, sisters, brothers, grandparents, teachers, pastors, and any other significant people in your childhood, then record your reactions and lead you back to these feelings as you pray.

If you do not feel God's promised peace—if you have headaches, muscle spasms, or stomach problems, or if you have low energy, frequent depression, or a pervasive feeling of fear or self-doubt—perhaps there's someone you haven't forgiven. Maybe it's *you*. Don't stuff these disquieting thoughts away to add to your stress level; deal with them. Begin by asking God to make you open to His direction and willing to hear His voice. "God is always at work in you to make you willing and able to obey his own purpose" (Philippians 2:13 TEV).

When Lana and those she has trained spend a day with an individual in need, they explore the childhood relationships and are alert to consistent types of conflicts or repeated habit patterns. They take notes throughout the questioning time and pray quietly and constantly for wisdom. The Lord always sorts out their jots and tittles and gives them direction in which to pray.

Seamands, who is a professor at Asbury Seminary, says that this time of searching for insights "is often necessary to uncover the hidden hurts, the unmet needs, and the repressed emotions which are preventing us from getting to the truth which will set us free."[6]

Following the counseling comes the time of prayer. For me the counseling was eight hours with Lana followed by five hours of prayer. If anyone had told me before that I could pray for five hours, I would not have believed it, and yet the time flew as if it were minutes as the Holy Spirit ministered to me in a healing of some past hurts and rejections and in a forgiveness of some people I hadn't previously felt deserved forgiveness. For more of my personal experience read my chapter on "Pains of the Past" from *Lives on the Mend*.

Seamands in his *Healing of Memories* states:

> In this special prayer, we allow the Spirit to take us back in time to the actual experience and to walk through those painful memories with us. It is then . . . that we pray as if we were actually there at the time it took place, allowing God to minister to us in the manner we needed at that time.
>
> This prayer time is the very heart of the healing of memories. It is in prayer that the healing miracle begins; without it, the whole process may simply be a form of autosugges-tion, catharsis, or feeling therapy. This special

time of prayer cannot be bypassed, if there are
to be lasting results. . . . Then, during the time
of prayer, the Spirit peels away that layer and
opens us up to deeper levels of our own
minds and helps us *to discover what the real
issue is.*[7]

We must remember that whether we spend time in
prayer alone, with a friend, or with a skilled counselor,
our basic purpose is to find the real issue behind our
present pain so that we may deal with it effectively and
be set free. We are not aiming for emotional experiences
or to join ourselves with some self-appointed guru but
to strip away the Band-Aids we've placed over our
wounds and clean them out, with or without the help
of a professional counselor. When we hold our aim
clearly in mind, we will not be led into therapy that
is contrary to Scripture.

As I have watched Lana and her Philippian Ministries
staff work quietly and patiently with the scores of
women and a few men that I have sent to them, I have
been overwhelmed with the power that God has to
change lives.

I'm sure there are as many different ways of praying
as there are people who pray, but since I am most
familiar with how Lana handles the prayer session, let
me recount what she does as a potential guideline for
you or the friend/counselor working with you.

Renounce any past occult involvement, including
horoscopes, Ouija boards, fortune-tellers, and cult
memberships.

Praise God for who He is and for sending His Son,
Jesus, to die for our sins and set us free. Claim the power
of the Holy Spirit in the revelation of our new and
cleansed life.

Move through life's events in chronological order, whether you are by yourself or are being led through the prayer time by another person. Pray over every hurt and rejection, and realize the Lord Jesus forgiving you and helping you to forgive others.

Forgive anyone whose face comes before you during the prayer time, and ask God to restore you to fellowship even if you may never see that person again. Unforgiveness eats away only at the person clinging to it.

Fight the spiritual battle by renouncing any satanic thought which occurs. Label it and send it on its way.

Forgive your family members of any past hurt, recent rejection, or traumatic event for which you feel they are even slightly responsible.

Seek out in prayer any people who have hurt you by asking the Lord to let you see them through His eyes. Free them from your underlying judgment.

Thank God that nothing you've been through is wasted and pray that He will redeem the years that the locusts have eaten.

Close by placing the pieces of your life into the hands of Jesus as you would a puzzle and asking Him to put it all together until it begins to make sense.

These steps and suggestions are helpful for anyone but are especially necessary for a person who has unexplainable symptoms and has been unable to find answers. God is open and available to heal His crippled children.

For information on any of the types of counseling mentioned, call our office at (714) 888-8665.

I have tried in this revision of *Blow Away the Black Clouds* to present the problem of depression and provide a variety of solutions. Some are specific things we can do ourselves. Some are suggestions for physical changes or medical checkups. Some are preventive, as in teen depression and suicide. Some are spiritual steps accompanied by appropriate sample prayers. Some open our minds that we might have a healing of memories.

No one person will need all of these, but I have laid out for your consideration those methods that I have seen produce results. Some of you may ask, "Isn't going to church and being a good Christian enough?"

In *Today's Christian Woman* Evelyn Minshull writes:

> There is the classic Christian response, of course—a valid answer often offered with glib assurance by those who've never walked the dark pathways of depression. Quoting David, they direct the sufferer to God—with a blissful unawareness that depression often includes an inability to sense the presence of God, to warm to His healing and love.[8]

Hopefully, for most of us being a Christian is enough, but for those of you who are in constant pain or are deeply depressed, you may need some special help to blow away that big black cloud.

15

'Tis the Season to Be Jolly!

A few years ago I was asked to be on a nationally televised talk show on "Christmas Depression." While at the beauty shop having my nails done in preparation for the taping, I mentioned where I was going and the subject I was to discuss. Without my even asking, women started offering their opinions. One lady in her sixties said, "I get depressed every Christmas because I can't do what I used to do and entertain the whole family. I have to go to my daughter's house, and she's in charge."

A young college girl added, "I get depressed because I'm at an in-between age. I'm not a child but I don't have a home of my own. I guess I just don't fit anywhere." She also told me that her college had so many students like her that they were having a special seminar on holiday depression.

One of the beauticians said she had been in the May Company and they were doing a survey with the holiday shoppers. Each person was asked: "Do you have a charge account here? What is your favorite store?

Was the help here polite to you? What is your biggest problem at this season?'' The girl had answered the questions and then asked the surveyor what he found the biggest problem to be. His answer was, "Ninety percent of all the people I've talked to are depressed."

A businesswoman came out from under the dryer and said, "It's in-laws! They're the big problem! Each family insists that you have Christmas with them. It's some sort of popularity contest, and whichever one you don't go to hates you. I don't know whether to eat two dinners or no dinners."

Without going further than the beauty shop, I had a cross section of women's attitudes about Christmas depression, all of which I was able to quote on TV.

That same week a local station did a five-part series on holiday depression on their eyewitness news entitled "Silent Nights, Lonely Nights." Later Phil Donahue had a show on the same subject in which he happily egged everyone on to vent their feelings about the emotional crisis of Christmas.

Why are people especially upset in the season that's supposed to be jolly? Why when bells are ringing and carols singing do we sit in silence? Why when there's mistletoe hanging everywhere is no one kissing us?

One reason is that our expectations are too high. We've watched too much TV where everyone is in a designer gown at an elaborate banquet in a castle. We've leafed through too many magazines where ordinary housewives have made gingerbread houses that Hansel and Gretel could both live in. We've gone to the church craft class and see other people make Christmas trees out of tuna fish cans while we've glued ourselves to a pine cone and spilled sticky glitter to both knees.

"Everyone else is having fun and I haven't been

invited to one party, made one cookie, or decorated one wreath.'' Somehow we get an inflated idea of what the season to be jolly is supposed to be, and when jolly turns to folly, we get depressed.

''The mismatch between the way life is and the way we'd like it to be becomes more exaggerated during the holidays,'' said Dr. Allan J. Comeau, a training officer for the San Bernardino County Department of Mental Health.[1]

The advent of Christmas throws our thoughts back to our youth, a memory which in itself could be depressing for those who had traumatic circumstances. For those who have recollections of fun times in the snow and lavish dinners with the family by the fire and are now divorced in Dallas, Christmas day can be depressing.

If you've lost a loved one in the past calendar year, the thought of a Christmas without that special angel at her spot at the table can be overwhelming. For the elderly or ill, Christmas can start them brooding over whether they'll be around next year.

Joel Sorum, executive director of the Mental Health Association of San Bernardino, stated:

Christmas represents a passage. We think about how fast the year has gone, and of all the things we didn't accomplish. We think of past Christmases and the people who aren't with us any longer, because of death, or divorce, or because the children are gone and have families of their own. It stirs up very basic deep feelings, and it's particularly difficult for people who are divorced or separated, or elderly, or disabled—people who are the least anchored.[2]

For those who are in financial straits, Christmas seems fun only for the rich: "Everyone has plenty of money but me." Some people get depressed when they can't buy lavish gifts while others charge up a storm and postpone their depression until the bills come in later.

Let's say that for any of these reasons, or for some creative ones of your own, you get depressed at holidays. What can you do about it?

Face the problem before it appears. Sit down and make a realistic appraisal of what went wrong last year and how you can prevent it this year. Did you blow up at your family because you were overtired? Were you angry because you didn't get what you had asked for? Was there a fight over where to be on Christmas Eve? When you look back on it, wasn't most of it trivial?

> Mental-health specialists say that the problem is a cumulative malaise that is rooted in poor planning, unrealistic expectations, and a melancholic sense of *tempus fugit*.
>
> The symptoms frequently include an overbooked social calendar, overspent budget, and overindulgent imagination.[3]

Plan ahead. Why not have a gathering of the key relatives in October and ask what each one is planning for the holidays? While eating your food in your home, they will be hard-pressed to fight you over who serves Christmas dinner. You have to go into this session with an open mind and be happily willing to do it their way. You may become a mediator for the others, but whatever happens when Christmas arrives, you will be harmless and blameless. If you can have a sweet spirit of conciliation and know that it doesn't really matter whose plates you eat from, you could be the catalyst for true peace on earth and goodwill toward men.

Divide responsibilities. In our family we rotate whose home we go to for Christmas Eve, breakfast, presents, and dinner. We plan ahead and divide the responsibilities for the food preparation. The hostess usually does the turkey and potatoes, with others bringing a vegetable, salad, or dessert. With this apportioning of duties, one person is not the depressed drudge of the day and yet no one has to do too much. Don't be a Christmas martyr mother.

Make it simple. When I was a child, Christmas and Thanksgiving brought forth every vegetable ever grown, each served in its own bowl. By the time we finished dinner we were overstuffed and overwhelmed with the amount of dishes we had to wash. I've found that we can have a dinner without 12 vegetables and with the plates served up in the kitchen, thereby eliminating all serving pieces but the carving board. The food, fun, and fellowship flow freely, and no one minds when the cleanup is simple. Don't exhaust yourself over impressive gourmet treats and lavish displays, with everyone so tense that they want to leave before the flaming plum pudding.

Do for others. Don't get so caught up in elaborate and time-consuming preparation that you don't have time for *people.* If Christmas cards are a problem, don't send them until after the holidays, as I did this year. The recipients have more time to read them when the rush is over. Call some friends far away and let them know you're thinking of them. Send a poinsettia to a shut-in. Give some gifts to the poor.

In the mall in our town a list was put up of children in need, with their ages and first names. My two grandsons took money they had in the bank and bought specific presents for two other boys. They helped Lauren wrap them and brought them to the mall. Lauren took the time to teach them the true spirit of Christmas giving.

My friends Betty Lou and Mildred are both widowed, and they chose to spend their money on a family in Mexico and not on each other. They bought gifts for all the children and sent them ahead. They had a quiet Christmas day together, knowing they had made a poor family happy.

Remember the reason. Was Christmas created for presents and parties or for the celebration of our Savior's birth? Even evangelical Christians get so caught up in the commercial aspect of the season that they forget the reason. My daughter Lauren has an empty manger surrounded by straw on the dinner table for the month of December. Each time one of the boys does a spontaneous good deed he gets to put a piece of straw in the manger in preparation for the birth of Jesus. On Christmas Eve they put the baby Jesus into the manger and celebrate with a cake that says "Happy Birthday, Jesus!"

When our attention is focused on the true reason for Christmas we won't be depressed when we aren't invited to enough parties. When we're giving to others in Jesus' name, He will give us peace that passes all understanding.

Minister to those who have lost loved ones in the past year. The first Christmas is always the hardest for someone grieving over a death while everyone else seems to be at a perpetual party.

Compassionate Friends, an organization composed of parents who have lost a child, starts in October preparing families for the holidays. They say that Halloween is often the trigger for seasonal depression as parents see the neighborhood children in costume coming to the door for treats. They automatically remember the year that Junior was Superman or Sally was the Great Pumpkin.

As other families seem to anticipate the feast of Thanksgiving and the joy of Christmas, the grieving family tends to withdraw with dread. Remember them, and include them in some meaningful activity, being careful not to bemoan your own trivial problems. I recall how upset I was after losing my two sons when a friend came over in tears because her eighth-grader had to get glasses!

Compassionate Friends understands the emotions of those in grief, and a local chapter has an open house for its members between Christmas and New Year's called the "Thank Heaven We Survived the Holidays" party.

Marilyn Heavilin, one of our CLASS speakers and the subject of Chapter 12 in *Lives on the Mend*, gave birth to twins on Christmas morning. Ethan died of pneumonia when he was ten days old and Nathan was killed by a drunk driver when he was 17 years old. For Marilyn and her husband Christmas is difficult every year.

> Ethan's death was a great loss and disappointment to us, but since we still had Nate's birthday to celebrate on Christmas day we managed through the holidays quite well. However, after Nathan was taken from us, my excitement about Christmas was gone. As I remembered his last birthday—the friends who were there, the gifts he received, the fun we had, how proud we were of him—my dread of celebrating Christmas without him began to build.

I wanted to ask God to cancel December—we would try it again the next year. The thought of enjoying Christmas carols, decorations, gifts, and family gatherings seemed inconceivable without my precious Nate.

One day while browsing in a bookstore I was leafing aimlessly through a display of posters when a particular one caught my attention. It was the picture of a beautiful red rose, the dewdrops glistening on its petals. The tears streamed down my face as I read the quote at the bottom of the poster:

GOD GIVES US MEMORIES SO WE
MIGHT HAVE ROSES IN DECEMBER

Roses in December! Could God really do that for me? I asked Him to show me the roses in my December: The note on the Christmas tree stating that my daughter and her husband vowed to give something to a needy person each Christmas in memory of their brother, the 25 friends who gave up their family gatherings to spend Christmas day with us, the bouquets of roses I received, the friends who called to say, "I remember what day this is and I'm praying for you," the friend who sent a card which read "To Comfort You At Christmas," and the very special friends who hugged me and didn't rebuke me when I cried.

Each year my husband Glen and I try to reach out to others in special ways—sending a boy to basketball camp or giving money to a local hospice in memory of Nate. I have collected "To Comfort You At Christmas" type cards to send to those who have been recently bereaved, and I keep looking for the roses.

The day of our CLASS staff Christmas brunch at my home, I looked out the window and saw one red rose alone on a bush. I picked it and put it in a bud vase by Marilyn's place, giving her a memory of roses in December.

Are you giving roses in December to your friends in need? Or are you so encumbered by your own burdens that you can't see beyond your own tree? Well-meaning Christians sometimes forget what the season of giving is really all about.

Marilyn concludes:

> Actual roses will fade, wither, and turn to dust, but roses in the form of precious memories or faithful friends are a soothing balm to the hurting heart and will last forever as precious roses in December.

Some people are so determined to make this Christmas the best ever that the pressure of preparation and performance have them exhausted before the festive day. Competition drives others to distraction: I will bake better brownies than anyone in the "cookie exchange;" I will wrap all my gifts in gold foil and they'll know which are mine; I will put up more lights than anyone on the street.

Isn't it amazing how the celebration of the birth of our Lord Jesus brings out for some of us the baser qualities of greed, self-pity, and competition, followed closely by disappointment and depression? Our eyes seem to focus on parties we're not going to, gifts we're not able to buy, and lights that have lost their twinkle.

I had an opportunity to reflect on how many people are out looking for colored lights, for some sparkle in the night, for some glimpse of the star in the East when I arrived at Heritage USA two weeks before the Christmas of 1985.

As I was chauffeured onto the grounds of the impressive headquarters for the PTL Ministries, I was amazed at the long line of cars backed up for miles to the freeway exit waiting for dark to come so they might drive through Christmas City and view—in awe—over 1,250,000 lights artistically placed on the endless stretch of holiday decorations.

We drove through a tunnel of twinkling arches that would put McDonalds to shame, down Candy Cane Lane, through Sugar Plum Valley, up Angel Boulevard, and to the lake surrounded by a fence of festive lights.

As we approached the Heritage Grand Hotel, the limousine door was opened by a costumed attendant who looked as if he had just danced out of the cast of *The Nutcracker Suite*. It was all perfect!

In the elegant lobby I saw a massive Christmas tree that rose three stories high, dwarfing the two fountains and the hundreds of people. I was thrilled to find that my room on the second floor overlooked a Main Street like the one at Disneyland and that from my balcony I could view the people wandering in and out of the Victorian-style shops, eating popcorn from the huge machine below my window and dining at the Grand Promenade Cafe.

I could hear the harpist accompanied by the lady at the golden grand piano, alternating with the strolling minstrels singing carols. Scrooge himself could get excited over Christmas City USA, where every detail exceeded the memories of Christmas past and the dreams of Christmases to come.

As I sat in my room, waiting to speak at the Christmas banquet and be on the Jim Bakker television show, I began to wonder about all those people out there in their cars lining up early for their drive to view the lights of Christmas.

Who are they? Who are the million people who visit each season? Are they all happy? Or are some of them perhaps depressed?

Are there some families seeking something meaningful to bind them together for another tenuous year?

Are there some lonely people who came without friends in hopes that the lights would brighten up their lives like magic?

Are there some who see Christmas as only Santa and snowflakes?

Are there elderly couples with tearful memories of happier holidays of the past?

Are there some children looking out at the lanes of candy canes and wondering silently why Daddy won't be home this Christmas?

Yes, who are these people waiting each night in their cars?

What will they do when the line starts to move?

Some will read the pamphlet handed to them by a girl in a swirling red cape at the front gate inviting them to stop and visit.

Some may attend the nightly musical, *The Birthday Party*, that answers the question, spelled out in lights throughout the route, "What can we give the King?"

Some may sign up for the daily multitude of seminars and Bible studies offered by PTL. Some may be spiritually uplifted by the message from the singing Christmas tree. Some may seek counsel; some may converse with the costumed staff; some may sit alone on the bench below my window and eat popcorn.

But a large number of these people will just drive through and never get out of their cars. Many will stay within the protective walls of their vehicle, afraid to step out and be vulnerable. Some may open the window a crack to catch the chorus of a carol. Many will look at the lights from a distance, hoping somehow to be touched and transformed by a twinkle.

Many will never get to the bookstore for a Bible or to Main Street to mingle with the other men and women. Many will taste only a touch of the season through tinted glass, for there's no time to open the door or there's fear of what might be on the other side. Many are driving cars of care, and they don't dare to get out.

There are many people around each one of us each season who won't get out of the car, some who won't even open the window an inch to let the music bring melody to their lives or to listen to a message that might bring relief to the monotony of the moment.

It's easy to miss those who are driving through town with the windows up and the doors locked. It's hard to look for the person hiding in the backseat of life behind a barrier of loneliness and pain.

While we may stand with meaning at the manger, many are moving by just looking at the lights. Are we willing to turn from our festivities and help someone out of the car? Are we willing to lend a hand of assistance and an invitation to open the door of their hearts to Jesus as He says, ''Behold I stand at the door and knock; if anyone opens the door, I will come in''?

Let's not miss the opportunity of offering an open door to those waiting in line hoping to get a glimpse of Christmas as they drive slowly through our town.

Let's help them get out of the car and hear the music,

for the best way to lift our own spirits is to lead another person to our Lord, to put our eyes on Jesus, the Author and the Finisher of our faith. If Christmas has you down, perhaps your focus is on the lights and not the Light. Perhaps you are like those people in the long line of cars waiting for some external circumstances to brighten up your life, hoping that the decorations will decrease your depression.

Take your eyes off yourself
And next year remember
You can be God's hand
To give out roses in December.

NOTES

CHAPTER 2

1. David Brand, "Beyond the Blues," in *The Wall Street Journal*, Apr. 7, 1972.
2. Ibid.
3. Quentin Hyder, *The Christian's Handbook of Psychiatry*. Fleming H. Revell, Spire Books, 1973, p. 81.
4. *The Wall Street Journal*, Apr. 7, 1972.
5. Martin Seligman in *Psychology Today*, June 1973, p. 44.
6. *Newsweek*, Apr. 23, 1984.
7. Sam Keen, "Boredom," in *Psychology Today*.
8. "Half in Love With Easeful Death," in *Eternity*, Mar. 1985, p. 28.
9. Peter Saltzman in *Family Circle*, Apr. 1977.
10. *The Wall Street Journal*, Apr. 7, 1972.
11. *Psychology Today*, June 1973.
12. Brina Caplan, "Been Down So Long...," in *Savvy*, Feb. 1985, p. 81.
13. *Psychology Today*, June 1973.
14. "Suicide-Prone Patients: Warning Clues," in *Diagnosis*, Nov. 1984.

CHAPTER 3

1. Sandi Cushman in *The Los Angeles Times*, Dec. 15, 1976.
2. Spirit of Freedom Ministries, P.O. Box 50583, New Orleans, LA 70150.

3. Quentin Hyder, *The Christian's Handbook of Psychiatry.* Fleming H. Revell, Spire Books, 1973, p. 86.
4. Victor M. Victoroff in *Diagnosis*, Nov. 1984, p. 64.

CHAPTER 4

1. *The Wall Street Journal*, Apr. 7, 1972.
2. Robert Browning, "Man and Woman," Andrea del Sarto.
3. Proverbs 29:18.
4. Victor M. Victoroff in *Diagnosis*, Nov. 1984, p. 64.
5. *USA Today*, Oct. 21, 1985.
6. Betty Baye, "Incest, True Stories of Women Who Suffered and Survived," in *Beauty Digest*, Jan. 1985, p. 22.

CHAPTER 5

1. Frederic Flach, "The Secret Strength of Depression," in *Family Circle*, May 1978.

CHAPTER 6

1. Maxwell Maltz, *Psycho-cybernetics*, 1960, p. 106.

CHAPTER 12

1. *America's Health*, Vol. 6, No. 3, 1984.
2. Robert Frost, "Death of a Hired Man," 1914.
3. Terry McDermott, "God Comes Back," in *The Seattle Times Pacific*, Nov. 17, 1985.
4. Ibid.
5. Ibid.
6. Ibid.

7. *USA Today*, Mar. 29, 1985.
8. Beverly Beyette, "Teen-agers' No. 1 Drug: Alcohol," in *The Los Angeles Times*, Sept. 18, 1983.
9. Ibid.
10. Ibid.
11. Ann Landers, "What Are You Afraid Of?" in *The San Bernardino Sun*, Dec. 14, 1985.
12. James G. Fudge, *The Drug Crisis*. The Spirit of Freedom, P.O. Box 50583, New Orleans, LA 70150.
13. Ann Landers, "Potential Suicide Victim Cries Out for Understanding," in *The San Bernardino Sun*, July 25, 1985.

CHAPTER 13

1. John H. Hewett, *After Suicide*.
2. Ann Landers in *The San Bernardino Sun*, May 7, 1985.
3. David Baldwin, "What You Can Do for the Family of a Teenage Suicide," in *Medical Economics*, Feb. 4, 1985.
4. Ibid.

CHAPTER 14

1. "Emotions Anonymous offers friendship to those seeking help," in *Austin American-Statesman*, Mar. 31, 1985.
2. David A. Seamands, *Healing of Memories*. Victor Books, 1985, p. 65.
3. Ibid., p. 38.
4. Howard Wolinsky, "Pains May Be Body Talking to the Mind," in *The Los Angeles Times*, Dec. 20, 1985.
5. Ibid.

6. Seamands, p. 24.
7. Seamands, p. 27.
8. Evelyn Minshull, "Shall We Pretend?" in *Today's Christian Woman,* July/Aug. 1984, p. 48.

CHAPTER 15

1. John Weeks, "Don't surrender to the ghosts of Christmas past," in *The San Bernardino Sun*, Dec. 13, 1981.
2. Ibid.
3. Jean Dietz, "Dark Side of the Holiday Season," in *The Los Angeles Times*, Dec. 25, 1983.

BIBLIOGRAPHY

BOOKS

Adams, Jay. *The Christian Counselor's New Testament*. Presbyterian and Reformed Publishing, 1977.

_____. *Competent to Counsel*. Presbyterian and Reformed Publishing, 1973.

Barnes, Emilie. *More Hours in My Day*. Eugene: Harvest House, 1982.

_____. *Survival for Busy Women*. Eugene: Harvest House, 1986.

Bateman, Lana. *God's Crippled Children*. Dallas: Philippian Ministries, P.O. Box 31122, 1985.

Brandt, Henry R. *The Struggle for Peace*. Wheaton: Scripture Press Publications, 1965.

Briggs, Lauren Littauer. *What You Can Say When You Don't Know What To Say*. Eugene: Harvest House, 1985.

Carlson, Dwight, M.D. *Run and Not Be Weary*. Old Tappan, NJ: Fleming H. Revell, 1974.

De Rosis, Helen A., M.D., and Victoria Y. Pellegrino. *The Book of Hope*. New York: Macmillan Publishing, 1976.

Glasser, William, M.D. *Reality Therapy*. New York: Harper & Row, 1965.

Haggai, John Edmund. *How to Win Over Worry*. Grand Rapids: Zondervan Publishing House, 1959.

Hyder, O. Quentin, M.D. *The Christian's Handbook of Psychiatry*. Old Tappan, NJ: Fleming H. Revell, Spire Books, 1971.

Littauer, Florence. *It Takes So Little to Be Above Average*. Eugene: Harvest House, 1983.

_____. *Lives on the Mend*. Waco: Word, 1985.

_____. *Out of the Cabbage Patch*. Eugene: Harvest House, 1984.

_____. *Pursuit of Happiness*. Eugene: Harvest House, 1978.

Littauer, Florence, and Marita Littauer. *Shades of Beauty*. Eugene: Harvest House, 1982.

Maltz, Maxwell, M.D. *Psycho-cybernetics*. New York: Essandess Special Editions, 1960.

Omartian, Stormie. *Greater Health God's Way*. Sparrow Press, 1984.

Roberts, Sam E., M.D. *Exhaustion: Causes and Treatment*. Emmaus, PA: Rodale Books, 1967.

Ross, Dr. Harvey, M.D. *Fighting Depression*. New York: Larchmont Books, 1975.

Seamands, David A. *Healing of Memories*. Wheaton: Victor Books, 1985.

Steincrohn, Peter J., M.D. *Low Blood Sugar*. Chicago: Henry Regnery, 1972.

Veninga, Robert. *A Gift of Hope*. Boston: Little, Brown and Company, 1985.

Watson, Dr. George. *Nutrition and Your Mind*. Harper & Row, A Bantam Book, 1972.

CASSETTES

Littauer, Florence. *Blow Away the Black Clouds*. Waco: Word, Inc.

_____. *Conquering Depression*. Waco: Word, Inc.

RESOURCES

Al-Anon Family Group Headquarters (For families of
  alcoholics)
One Park Avenue
New York, NY 10016

Alateen (For teenage children of alcoholics)
One Park Avenue
New York, NY 10016

Alcoholics Anonymous (For adult alcoholics)
P.O. Box 459
New York, NY 10163

Alive, Inc. (Suicide prevention)
12141 Lewis Street
Garden Grove, CA 92640

Alcoholics Victorious (A Christian support agency for
  alcoholics)
28 S. Sangamon Street
Chicago, IL 60607

Cenikor Foundation, Inc. (For drug addiction)
2209 South Main
Fort Worth, TX 76110

Compassionate Friends, Inc. (For parents who have lost
  a child)
P.O. Box 1347
Oak Brook, IL 60521

Empty Cradle (A support agency for parents experiencing
  miscarriage, stillbirth, and infant death)
6497 Decanture Street
San Diego, CA 92120

Institute for the Study of Sexual Assault
403 Ashbury Street
San Francisco, CA 94117

National Association on Drug Abuse Problems
355 Lexington Avenue
New York, NY 10017

National Center for the Prevention and Control of Rape
Parklawn Building, Room 15-99
5600 Fishers Lane
Rockville, MD 20857

National Coalition Against Sexual Assault
c/o Austin Rape Crisis Center
P.O. Box 7156
Austin, TX 78712

National Committee for Youth Suicide Prevention
230 Park Avenue, Suite 835
New York, NY 10169

National Federation of Parents for Drug-Free Youth
P.O. Box 722
Silver Springs, MD 20901

National Organization for Victim Assistance
P.O. Box 11555, Dept. BHG
Washington, D. C. 20008

Overeaters Anonymous
2190 West 190th Street
Torrance, CA 90504

Project COPE (A support group for parents experiencing
   stillbirth and infant death)
9160 Monte Vista Avenue
Montclair, CA 91763

Recovery Headquarters (A support agency for agoraphobics)
802 N. Dearborn Street
Chicago, IL 60610

Sexual Assault Research Association
P.O. Box 12951
Salem, OR 97301

The Spirit of Freedom (A Christian support agency for
   alcoholics)
P.O. Box 50583
New Orleans, LA 70150